New Rush: Diamond fever

Gert van Jaarsveld

CONTENTS

Chapter 1: The decision

"Fuck it!"

He tosses the hoe away as if it were a poisonous adder. It lands on its handle and jumps through the air landing five yards further.

"Shit!" Samuel moans and carefully licks the blister that has burst open in his hand and from which the salty fluid makes clear lines over his dirty hand palm.

"It is this damn handle. He refuses to buy new handles. See how the rough, homemade thing injured my hand!"

His brothers look at the young giant and laugh at the sudden outburst, but a whirlwind that has, in the meantime, gathered sand, throws it down on them. The sand burns in their eyes and hurts their sweaty faces.

"Let's rest for a while," giggles Chris. He looks over the dismal patch of plants that struggles to become mealies in this drought while the weeds flourish in between the sparse plants.

"The mealies must be hoed today," their stepfather ordered this morning, "after the rain, we won't be able to contain the weed."

The 'we' of course doesn't include himself. It is the work of his three stepsons. It is their payment for the goodness of his heart, for the enormous lot of food they devour, for free boarding and lodging.

"Why on earth you want to plant mealies in this arid earth is beyond me," says Herklaas while they are walking in the direction of a lonely camel thorn tree with sparse foliage and almost no shade.

"You can say that again," Chris concurs. "But you know it is only a way to pest us."

"I don't understand." Samuel is still licking

Sometimes Chris becomes annoyed to no end by his brother's stupidity. As strong as Samuel is, as stupid he can sometimes be.

Enraged Chris speaks; spittle spatters from his mouth.

"Don't you also fucking be so stupid! He doesn't grant us anything! We must work like slaves from dawn to dusk and often hear how thankful we should be for food in our stomachs and a roof over our heads. No, he grants us nothing; he and that little shit boy of his who sits with his ass in England!"

The two brothers know it is no time to argue with Chris. He is too furious. They sit down under the scant shade of the tree and drink warm water out of their water bottles.

"Look," says Samuel after quite a while, "I'm not going to hoe another inch of this damn land with that fucking thing. My hands are chafed raw by the rough wood of the handle!"

Chris eyes them questioningly. Maybe the time is ripe. He has been waiting a long time for a chance like this. Since he had seen the articles in the newspaper of the enormous riches on the diamond diggings, especially New Rush, his mind is in turmoil. Earlier they had known vaguely something about the diggings at the Vaal River, but the article about the guy who dug up a monster of a diamond, worth hundreds of pounds, ignited a fire in him that nothing can quell. Here they sit in misery and work their asses off; over there someone digs up a bright future! Even if they don't get a big diamond, even if they have to do other work than digging, it can't be worse over there than here on this damn farm.

"Listen, my brothers, I am going to talk to you in all earnest. How many years have we been on this farm?"

"Almost ten years," Herklaas answers quickly. He is the cleverest of them. "We came in 1862, June 1862. And it is now January 1872."

"Correct, and what do we have?"

"Nothing," Samuel again licks over the sore in his hand. "Nothing at all!" He studies the sore as if it is a jewel.

"That's right. And do you think we will have anything in five year's time?"

They don't understand his question, but he is satisfied. He has got their attention.

"What if he one day tell us to take our belongings and bugger off?"

They don't answer him. It is true. They have nothing, no share in the inheritance of the farm. The farm belongs to Philip junior, they know that.

"In other words, we are really working for the little shit. Each tree we plant, each mealie land we plough, each sheep we shear; we do it for the lord that sits with his ass in England pretending to study."

Again his brothers remain silent. They know it, but now the reality hits them distinctly.

"For how long must we be the little shit's slaves?"

Samuel has a heavy frown. He hasn't thought so deeply about this before. Chris is right, they are working like slaves but could get kicked off the farm at any moment.

"But …" Herklaas nervously tries to come in. He has already the feeling he will loathe the process which is unfolding here and which his thin nerves won't handle. He is afraid of new things.

"Think it over carefully. As soon as we have helped Philip junior to finish his studies, he can come and tell us to fuck off. And it is his full right. He is the boss of this farm. It was explained to us many times."

A nauseating feeling hits Herklaas' stomach. Samuel remains silent. He is still licking his sore hand absentmindedly as if he wants to lick it healthy like a dog licks his wounds.

Chris gets hold of a little stick and starts to draw little figures in the sand. He must now choose his words wisely.

"I propose we take our things and bugger off before someone else kicks us off."

It jerks in Herklaas's gut. Nausea pushes up in his throat. Samuel stops his licking and with a big frown on his face looks at Chris's slow movements.

"Shouldn't we get back to work?" Herklaas points to the land that is baking in the afternoon sun.

"We are not going to hoe and inch today. It is too hot for old big stomach to come and inspect. He will even not come tomorrow because he said he wants to go to Colesburg. And on Sunday we are gone!"

"S..Sunday," Herklaas stutters.

"Yes, Sunday." He has thought this through many times. Now is the moment.

"You've got a plan." Samuel sometimes can show considerable insight.

"I have a plan, yes. And we are going to talk it through and refine it."

Samuel grins. He hates all forms of farm work. To be rid of that!

"But we cannot leave just like this. What about mother's grave?"

It was sudden. Chris doesn't have an answer ready. Their father died when they were small boys. He was one of the trekkers who followed the Voortrekkers but near Colesburg he suddenly died. Heart attack. Their mother had to sell everything and had to hire lodgings in Colesburg. With washing and ironing for people, she had to clothe and feed her boys. They had almost nothing.

One day a rich farmer brought his trousers for alterations to fit his current corpulence. He looked at the boys, now teenagers, and did his arithmetic. His wife died soon after he had bought the farm near Philippolis for next to nothing and a barrel of cheap brandy from a Griqua. Yes, he indeed needed a woman's hand on the farm. And extra hands as well. Good workers were scarce. He proposed and she was delighted because everyone knew, Philip Shaw was stinking rich.

Philip Shaw brought four slaves home.

Their mother didn't last many years. Sick and overworked she attracted pneumonia five years ago. Philip Shaw refused to take her to the hospital in Colesburg and got an old Griqua woman to doctor her with herbs. It didn't help. One cold winter morning they buried her in the frozen earth on the farm.

It is Samuel who resolves this philosophically. "Mother isn't here anymore. She is there." He points with his forefinger skyward. "One day we will see her again." He looks up in the sky.

"But her grave," Herklaas desperately tries again, but his brothers know it is about the decision they have to make that frightens him to no end.

"You cannot sit at mother's grave for the rest of your life. And if old Thick One chases you off, you can't take the grave with you."

Chris is afraid he might have been too crass and continues soothingly.

"I know mother's grave is something we are clinging to and you were quite young when she departed, Herklaas. I know it is going to hurt you the most, but there is no other way. And now is our chance."

Samuel nods and moves a little back into the shade. He likes the plan even if there is no flesh on the bone yet. For hoeing and milking cows and dipping sheep and digging holes in the hard ground, he is more than fed-up. Furthermore, he is twenty-two, and when they once in a quarter attend church in Colesburg, the girls seem to get prettier and he dreams his days and nights away with magnificent, romantic notions.

Chris again scratches with his stick slowly in the sand. Late that afternoon the plan is refined and lazily they walk back to the farmhouse.

Chapter 2: Aletta

The donkeys are fatigued after the day's trek. Saltpetre covers their skins. They have moved so slowly and cumbersome through the veld following wagon spoors you can scarcely call a road, that they stop abruptly when Jasper screams for them to stop. Their heads are hanging low; the harnesses limp.

Aletta climbs down from the wagon. Earlier she has walked for hours next to the wagon to make the weight lighter, but late in the afternoon, she climbed on again, too tired and sunburnt to walk any further.

Her dad is like a lunatic. From the day he has heard about New Rush, nothing could stop him. And she must pay the price; and the donkeys. Their poor dog also. All along the great Gariep River on nearly impassable terrain. And now all along with one of the tributaries of the river, a few days travel from New Rush.

"They will need me. We can live comfortably there," he more than once convinced himself.

Jasper is a cobbler. He and his daughter trek from one farm to the other, from one missionary to the other, from town to town with his four lean donkeys and shabby wagon. Where he is allowed to stay over, he spans out and mends shoes, buys skins, and makes new shoes and sandals, but since the diamond glitter started to twinkle in his eyes, he mercilessly drives on inland.

Aletta knows the ritual. First, the donkeys are outspanned and knee-haltered. She takes the pots down and starts a campfire. As soon as it burns well, she puts the tripod over it and hangs a little pot over the fire. Then she begins with their meagre provision of greens brought along with great care, which she peels and put in a holder. Luckily she has two barrels of water which she had filled at the previous stop. The dog, Lion Head, already is flat on his stomach near a confusion of guinea fowls, motionless as if he is in a deep sleep. The guinea fowls are grazing undisturbed closer to him. The sun lies low on the horizon, a big orange ball, tired after his fiery day's work.

Suddenly the loud scream of a guinea fowl. Lion Head is already halfway on his way to the flock. The guinea fowls are still looking around to detect danger when he attacks the first one. He kills a nice fat one with one bite, and before the others can fly away, he jumps on a second one and grabs him by the neck. The fowl yells in agony for a moment. Then it is quiet.

Jasper walks up to the dog and gathers the fowls with a satisfied smile on his face. Lion Head barks excitedly and circles around him.

"Good work, Lion Head. Tonight is the night you and I are going to have a feast."

Downwind he slaughters the guinea fowls and takes off their feathers. The big one must go into the pot directly. The smaller one is hung by his bound feet at the wagon. It must also go into the pot later on. The fresh smell of meat and blood attracts predators. There are leopards in this region and also jackals and others raving for a bit of meat.

While Aletta cooks the guinea fowl and vegetables, it is time for him and his barrel. That is his great weakness, the barrels with cheap brandy. Cape Smoke they call it. Extremely potent. As a cobbler, he could live decently, but most of his money has gone through the barrel down his throat.

Aletta lights a lantern and hangs it near the fire on the wagon. Jasper gulps and gulps one big mouthful after the other out of his self-made tin cup and feels how the sense of well-being floods through him. One of these days he will be a rich man. New Rush will take care of that. Out of joy, he sings a few false notes. Aletta stands and stares at the sun that shows only its last slice. She knows how quickly the light can change into darkness after dusk. She checks the pot, stirs the coals a little and get her sleeping stuff from the wagon and make a bed under it.

Then she dishes up. Tin plates and forks, that's all that is left, except for a few spoons, of her mother's expensive cutlery. All of that has gone through the barrel like almost all their belongings.

She hates him. She hates to live with him. She hates his drinking, she hates it to look at the unkempt dirty figure. "Leave him," Jemima said to her at one of the missionaries, "let him struggle on his own. Why do you allow him to ruin your life?"

Leave him! She has considered this more than once and has made firm decisions but then she always saw the pale face of her mother on the white pillow in front of her. She then was sixteen.

Through the spasms of cough, her mother whispered hoarsely. "Don't leave him. Promise me!"

She averted her eyes because she already had a intense hatred for him for what he did to her mother because of his addiction. Her mother put her frail hand in hers.

"Promise me! You won't leave him! He can't survive on his own. He's like a little boy …"

"But why …?" She could not hide her bitterness.

"Because I love him. I love him more than I love my life! That's God's will. I can't help it. Don't leave him alone. Look after him."

Her eyes dimming already, begged. Aletta's inside shattered. She could only nod and started to cry. Her mother closed her eyes peacefully.

The gallop of a horse is a strange sound in the silence of dawn. It sounds as if it is coming nearer to them. Jasper jumps up hastily and hides his barrel. Then he fidgets around on the wagon and brings out his old front loader. Just to frighten someone. The thing is useless, hasn't fired in years and there is no gunpowder for it.

The rider comes into sight in the last twilight on the horizon near them. He stops for a while, but then the sound of the hoofs come nearer, the rider more easy-going this time. Near them he holds in the horse, let it walks nearer. In the light of the fire, he sees the old man and the young girl. The horse walks up to the wagon.

"Good evening. I am so glad to see people. I've been in the saddle the whole day. Uncle, may I unsaddle here for a while?"

He is a strong man with black hair and a neat moustache. His voice is strong and smooth.

"Good evening, Stranger," answers Jasper and puts his gun down. No need for this. The man looks neat enough and in one of his saddlebags, Jasper's keen eyes have already spotted what he dearly wants to see. "Yes, my man, take off the saddle. Where are you heading this time of night?"

The stranger jumps out of the saddle and comes closer with his hand outstretched. In the light of the fire, they can see him better. Neat, expensive clothes, neat waistcoat.

"I'm coming from New Rush," he says, while he shakes their hands. "Stefaans Verhoef is my name."

"Jasper Steenekamp and this is my daughter Aletta. Pleased to meet you, Stefaans."

Jasper is very jovial. He is already somewhat intoxicated from the brandy and now here is someone fresh from New Rush. What a lucky break!

"Get the man a veldstool to sit on, Aletta. And there is surely enough for him to eat in the pot."

"Thanks, Uncle. Maybe a little later. I earlier had biscuits and biltong. I'll quickly unsaddle my horse."

Stefaans has heard and seen enough. The old man has been looking into the bottle quite heavily, maybe the girl also. She is a lovely girl, with thin clothes that expose the full roundness of her femininity. He has been away from home for such a long time and he resisted getting intimate with the black prostitutes at New Rush. You never know what disease you can pick up from them.

He takes one of the bottles of brandy out of his saddlebag.

"You and I, Uncle, will have a nice, long chat," he says when he takes place on the stool.

"Yes, Stefaans. I want to hear everything about New Rush. I'm on my way there. Want to settle down there. I'm a cobbler, you know. Do you think there will be enough work for me?"

"For sure, Uncle. They swarm from all over the world to New Rush. Many feet must get shoes. Yes, you can make a good living there."

"That is what I reckon as well. Do you hear, Aletta?"

She doesn't react. She is only aware of the man's dark eyes that want to undress her. Tonight she will have to fend for herself. Katryn, an old Griqua woman warned her long ago.

"You are beautiful," she said, "very beautiful. But beauty can also be a burden. Men will all want to bed you. You will have to avoid them to give to the man you love that he is entitled to."

She didn't understand everything then but as the men have tried their luck with her, she became more vigilant. The man in front of her scares her to death.

"And you are on your way to where?"

"Deep in the Karoo, Uncle. We have a large sheep farm but the drought also hit us hard. My brother and I left the farm and bought a claim at New Rush. It is going well, but now I must go home to see if our people are all right. My brother remains at New rush in the meantime."

The bottle is nearing its end. Jasper's tongue drags heavily and Stefaans allows him to drink heavily. He only sips small quantities of the strong stuff but he drinks with his eyes.

"I'm going to bed. Night Father, goodnight, Mister Verhoef."

Her father nods but scarcely says anything. Stefaans rises and puts out his hand. Reluctantly she takes it. The little pressure he exerts is meaningful. She shivers. The last quarter moon shifts in behind a cloud. It is dark.

She listens to how they talk and talk. She hears how the man fetches another bottle. She listens to how her father's voice drags more and more. Then she falls asleep.

The jackal's call comes far and lonely. But it not what awakens her. It is the soft shuffle of feet next to her bed. In the background, she hears her father snores loudly. She reckons it could be past midnight.

She gets a fright when he softly whispers near her ear. Her inside clamps. She doesn't hear what he says. She only feels how his hand glides over her shoulder to her breast.

Chapter 3: Caprini

Caprini impatiently walks to and fro over the deck. He despises every moment of this boat trip. He hates the hoarse squawks of the seagulls that visit the ship from the shore to scavenge. He hates the waves that threaten to roll over the boat here on the east coast of Africa. He hates the high swells that toss the ship to and fro like a rubber plug. He hates it to stand on the front deck and to see the nose of the boat dips so that he only sees water and no air.

In his mind's eye, he sees the arid land of southern Italy, the chalk boulders amidst pale grass plains. Bright, blue skies, and solid earth. His stomach threatens to wash out his breakfast through his mouth. He breathes heavily and hates every moment. But he sticks it out. Caprini is a man who can persevere. In his neat tailor's suit and with his smooth combed hair and his aristocratic appearance he makes, although lean, an imposing impression. A rich businessman would be your first take of him.

And if you would talk to him and understands his crooked English, you would soon deduct a very clever one. And you won't know that just a month before he nearly lost his life because of the theft of gold; that he had to flee out of Canada to save his skin; that he had to spend a third of his fortune to pay Indians to smuggle him to the nearest port to catch a boat and to get away. You even won't' know that he, in an eye's wink and without remorse, betrayed his partner who now lodges in a frozen grave in Canada. Only if you look deep into his eyes and can detect something of his rockhard soul, you will understand something of this cruel, merciless man in front of you.

Caprini came out of the sludge of a pisspoor existence, had to sleep with the pigs in a sty, often had to eat with the pigs, and the teachers had to bathe him before they could allow him in class. He was ridiculed by the children so that his soul was misformed into hatred. He escaped that tosh existence by eloping. In Rome he had to carry stinking fish to survive, slept with the rogues and thieves, and eagerly absorbed all their cunning and shrewdness.

And when he, according to his judgement, was educated enough and had a little money, he went into the world following the sparkling gems and golden sands. It was where he believed money could easily be made. And money means power. With money you can buy your desires. Nothing, yes nothing, is more important than money.

The gold reefs of Canada attracted him first. On the boat, he met an Irishman with the same dreams like his. McDonald. Mac taught him basic English and told him what he knew about the panning of gold in the rivers, of getting a claim, the selling of the panned gold, or the exchange of gold for provisions. Mac's nephew delved somewhere in Canada and regularly wrote to Mac.

In late winter they trekked through the white Canada, all along the well-trodden paths, ate what there was, stayed hungry when there was no food, but every morning had gold in its mouth. After about a month's walking, they arrived at a little town at the goldfields. Their money was about spent, but they could afford a claim and basic equipment. They went to the claim and the delvers split their sides for these two imbeciles because it was the worst claim in the nearest hundred miles.

Mac dug and panned. He worked his fingers to the bone and luckily sometimes panned a little gold. Caprini just sat on a rock. He was planning. He studied the river carefully. In his head he calculated how much everyone panned and the profits they made. Brandy loosens tongues. There were a few big guys with several claims who employed workers. The workers could easily be bribed for a whiskey or two.

Day by day he scrutinized the flow of the river. Why do some get more gold than the others? The river flows with a wide curve. Their claim sat on the turn with a few rocks intruding into the water around which the water swirled. The real gold reef sat upstream somewhere, maybe in an obituary. The gold particles are flushed down the river. After days a theory started to form in his brain.

Mac was fed-up because he had to pan the whole day while Caprini just sat on his behind. After a month he began to moan.

"Don't worry. Tonight when they are all asleep we will pan a lot of gold."

"We'd better, or I'll kick your bloody ass."

Late that night Caprini lit the lantern, took a shovel and the pan, and walked to the rocks. Next to the rock, he tried what he had figured out. The water was slightly deeper at the swirl around the rock and the sand seemed simply a part of the rock, but if you looked carefully, you could see that the swirl of the water pushes the sand in a heap around the rock.

Mac, still half asleep, joined him.

"Take the lantern."

"You are as mad as a hatter!"

"Maybe I am."

He shoveled deep into the sand heap and panned it. Nothing. And another. Nothing.

"You are madder as a hatter."

"I've seen madder guys in my time."

Half of the sand heap around the rock was gone. Another time he dug deeply. When the water drained away with the sand, they were there, shining in the dim light of the lantern, unmistakably gold nuggets, a whole handful.

"You are not mad," Mac was flabbergasted. He wanted to shout out loud, but Caprini warned him.

"Not a word. I've got a plan."

They shoveled deep around the rock and discovered layers of gold. It was simple logic. When the current was stronger, it swirls around the rock and left the heavy gold behind. When the current subsides, the gold was buried under finer sand.

That night they panned more gold than other guys got in a month.

"No word, Mac. And we don't sell it soon."

Night after night they delved around the rock and got hands full of gold. During the day they remained in their tent and only for the show, Mac went to the claim late in the afternoon and shoveled further away from the rock, to no avail. The delvers laughed in their rough beards. These two guys wouldn't last long. For a few weeks, they carried on like this.

During the night they stripped the sandbank clean to get every morsel that had been brought by the swirl around the rock and only when it was in their pouches, it was time to execute Caprini's plan.

Friday, late in the afternoon. Mac shovelled nearer to the rock again to no avail. Caprini came closer to him with his pan. With his back towards the other, he carefully poured some gold in Mac's pan. He closed the pouch and hid it under his jacket. He nodded. It was time.

They started to scream and jumped like Indians in an exuberant dance in the shallow water. Mac poured half of his gold into Caprini's pan when they were sure they had the attention of their neighbours.

"We've got it!" Mac yelled. "We've got the best claim in this whole river!"

Inquisitively they came and had a look.

"Two shovels and two pans. And just look here!" Caprini tossed his cap into the air. "We've shovelled too far away from the rock. All the gold is here in this sandbank!"

The news ran down the river like water during a flood. The canteen was full of delvers when the two enters it looking quite important.

"Tonight you must drink only a little but pretend to indulge heavily. More water than whiskey, right, but talk loud as if you are drunk. I've already replenished our provisions. Tomorrow we are gone."

Mac didn't understand Caprini's plan fully. However, he was so glad about the gold, he didn't care. He had learned Caprini was shrewder than the other crooks and that he would make the best of the situation. He trusted Caprini completely.

Mac had to repeat the story over and over in his loud voice. They had never believed there was gold near the rock and in vain panned in the gravel away from it. The alcohol flowed and the guys were happy.

The time was ripe.

"From tomorrow onwards we are going to pan bags of gold." Caprini took out a pouch and waves it through the air. "If we could get this much in one day, we are going to get a lot from tomorrow on." He tapped with his forefinger on the bulging pouch.

"No, you are not!"

The big Greek's red face shone round and rough in the lantern lights. His long hair hung unkempt over his shoulders. His hands clamped open and close as if he was touching a hot iron. Suddenly it was dead quiet in the canteen.

"Of course we are!" Mac tried to stand up from his stool but a big hand pushed him back.

Caprini carefully approached them. He had seen the big man and had heard a lot about him. He had quite a few claims and a lot of workers. He was quite successful as well. He saw how the Irishman got utterly annoyed, red in the face, and tried to get up again.

"And why won't we?" Caprini tried to sound as light-hearted as possible, but his knees began to wobble.

"Because I say so!" His voice bellowed through the canteen's utter silence. Suddenly all the delvers were on the edge of their stools. Nice, a fight when the boys are drunk. Caprini watches him carefully. Mac just sat dead still, unsure whether he should tackle the big body in front of him. He opened his mouth, but Caprini gestures that he should shut his trap.

"And why would you, Sir, then want to say something like this?" He hopes his English and intonation is good enough for the Greek to interpret it as a friendly question.

The Greek keeps quiet for quite a while. He considered Caprini's tone of voice. This was the game he always enjoyed. He decided it was not sarcastic or challenging. He started laughing out loud and grabs a bottle of whisky from the bar. With a few gulps, a quarter of the bottle went through his throat. Then he was silent for quite a while, looking around the canteen at the delvers.

"He asks why I would say something like this!" he roars addressing the delvers while ignoring Caprini. "I will tell you why!" He again took a mighty swig from the bottle.

"Yes, I will tell you. It is because they are going to sell the claim to me right now!"

Chapter 4: Happy birthday, Dad!

Sunday is a clear, cloudless day. A good day to have a birthday. A long, idle day awaits him. Philip Shaw rubs his stomach. Ragie, his Griqua housekeeper, will have something special on this day. She has a knack with cooking that even the two women in his life never had even if she is simple in her head. A beautiful, young girl. He is even more content when he enters the kitchen. He can see when looking at the milk buckets that milking was done meticulously. Yes, he contemplates proudly, punctuality should be one of a successful farmer's important qualities.

Ragie has indeed prepared an exceptional breakfast and greedy he sits down. The trio comes in and friendly greet and convey their heartiest wishes with his birthday. They throw in words like mean a lot to them and looking after them so well.

After breakfast, he wants to walk around on the farm to check if everything has been done as ordered, but the sun is now blazing down. He retires to the veranda with reading material. He reads Philip junior's letter a few times. His heart fills with pride. A good son of his, this Philip junior! He is doing excellent in his studies at the university. He befriended quite nice mates. His father's money and contacts definitely played a major role. He visited family still in England. They were quite happy to see him and send their best wishes. It's only money that is a little bit on the short side. He would have liked to see more of England and before he returns also tour Europe. Philip senior smiles broadly. He knows his son's love for cash and forgives him the white lie wholeheartedly. One of these days he will sell a few sheep and send the money over.

Ragie is exhilarated to no end before lunch. She is humming all the time while she is cooking the food. So much money for so much pleasure! She never has thought it would befall her. Shaw is no one to wear his feelings on his sleeve and almost every day she has to endure his scathing tongue, but Chris has painted another picture. Shaw only speaks harshly to her because he likes her so much. If this were not the case, he wouldn't even have noticed her. It is his nature. It must be her and Chris' secret, but this afternoon after lunch …

She turns the succulent leg of lamb again to roast it golden brown. He loves it so much.

The trio helps to lay the table.

"Glasses?" Chris asks.

"In the sideboard." Ragie eyes widen. The utensils in the sideboard are out of bounds. Chris winks at her and she relaxes.

Eventually, the food is ready and dished up in bowls. They call Shaw where he is taking a nap on the veranda.

He frowns when he sees the glasses, but Chris is quick to explain.

"I took out the bottle of brandy. It is such a special day. We want to celebrate with you, dad." He accentuates the word dad.

At first, Shaw feels annoyed, but when he looks at the smiling faces of the three brothers and also Ragie that peeps naughtily at him, his heart softens. They are all he has one this lonely farm. Chris pulls out a chair for him.

"Come, sit down, Dad. I'll pour a tot and then Ragie can dish up."

He throws a stiff measure for Shaw but only wet their glasses. Then he fills the glasses with cold water.

They are ready to eat.

"We hope you are going to have a wonderful year. And I hope you will never forget this day!" Cris says with a broad smile.

They clink glasses and drink. Philip Shaw is mildly affected. He knows the boys can't take him and there is little love lost for them from his side. It is only that they are hands on the farm. But now, maybe he shouldn't be so hard on them. Suddenly he wishes that Philip junior could be here with them.

He empties his glass. Eagerly Chris tops it up, this time with more brandy than water. Ragie fills his plate to the brim with all his favourites. He eats with fat drooping from the sides of his mouth. A wonderful feeling of contentment fills his heart and jovially he talks about his plans with the farm. Ragie fills his plate again and again and Chris pours more brandy, each time more brandy, and less water.

He nearly couldn't get to his sleeping room. This is the best he has felt for a long time. He needs a bed. Not to sleep, but to rest his relaxed body. The curtains are closed and the room is not that hot. He strips off all his clothes and lies down on the bed. Now he feels he needs a woman. The brandy causes him to doze off.

Chris smiles at Ragie when the bedroom door closes.

"He is waiting for you, Ragie."

She wipes with the damp cloth over her face. She is excitedly breathing heavily. Chris gives her some money which she carefully hides somewhere in her clothing.

He gestures to the door. She unbuttons her frock from the top so that some of her breasts show clearly. Satisfied Chris smiles. He pushes her softly to the door. Ragie smiles broadly. So much money for so much pleasure. When she enters, she sees him naked on the bed. Such a naughty man, such a vagabond! She undresses and lies down next to him.

He only vaguely becomes aware of the woman that caresses him like in a dream.

Chapter 5: Horrifying events

"Aletta." He whispers softly and pushes with his palm against her breast.

"No, not now," she replies straight away. "It's that time of the month." She takes his hand and forces it away from her breast. Then she turns and pulls herself in a bundle like a hedgehog.

For a moment she feels his hand against her back, and then it is gone. Then he swears. She hears his footsteps on the grass. A while later she hears the loud noises of his horse's hoofs galloping away in the moonlit night.

Thanks, Katryn. Thank you so much!

The morning sun first crawls sleepily over the horizon. His friendly rays twinkle on the grass wet with dew. It plays over the lizards that lick water from the blades. It is quiet around the wagon. The donkeys graze nearby under a few camel thorn trees. Then she hears her father stirs and suddenly his loud snoring cuts through the air. It is the vulgar sounds of a man that has seen the bottom of nearly two bottles of brandy. He lies like a dead man next to the dead fire. She stands up and looks at him. She simply loathes him. Would he be concerned if the stranger raped her? He simply wouldn't know or care!

The Cape cobra is annoyed. It is hungry. It hasn't had a good night. It sails out from under a big rock and lies baking in the morning sun. A spiteful gad-fly is pestering him. Maybe an early mouse will pass by. The snake wriggles himself into the sand for camouflage. Then it lowers its head and waits.

Aletta isn't hungry. Her dad, in any case, will sleep for another few hours. She walks in the direction of the river. Just before the decline to the river down under, is the flat rock like a stool ready to be sat on. She leisurely approaches the rock while looking at the insects in their myriads now enjoying the early morning. She hears the pheasants and guinea fowls' loud cries. She sees the birds fluttering trough he air catching whatever insects they find. She eventually takes place on the rock eyeing the rising sun. Soon its friendly rays will change to heatwaves. It will lick up all the moisture that now glitters like diamonds on the stems and blades as he takes control of every nook that isn't in a shade. An hour or so from now it will bake down on the dry earth in all its ferocity and scorches the stones and rocks fiery hot.

She looks down at the river. It lies like a big shining snake peacefully in the morning sun. A big, sleeping, winding strip between green banks.

The cobra moves slightly when she takes place. She doesn't bother him because she is not food.

For a very long time, she sits dreaming on the rock. What will the near future hold in stall? She also is slightly excited about New Rush. At least they can stay there for quite a while. Maybe she can find work there. At least there are other people. They say it is an interesting lot of people. Boers, English, blacks, Griquas, brown people, and foreigners from all parts of the world.

A long time passes. Then she hears her father call from the wagon. He has awakened earlier than usual, she thinks. She doesn't answer. Give him time to awake fully. She feels irritated that her peaceful moments are interrupted, but after her father has urinated he lies down and is soon fast asleep.

She walks back to the wagon and organizes everything. The rest of the guinea fowl she puts in a smaller holder and also a few biscuits. She took off the donkeys' knee halters and walks to a big camel thorn tree with crochet. The day lazily advance towards noon. The sun now is directly shining from above, a fiery ball.

Later she walks down to the rock again. The distant river lying so peacefully has its own attraction. She thinks about the millions of drops that together stream down to the sea. Then she just sits on the rock, thinking of nothing else.

This time Jasper has awakened fully. He quenches his thirst from the brandy bottle that has a few drops left. He screams at Aletta and she screams back. He walks towards her swinging from one side to the other still highly intoxicated. He stops, takes the last swig from the bottle, and throws it down. He stumbles over low shrubs and starts to talk incoherently about New Rush and the money he is going to make.

Next to the rock he trips and falls down. The cobra's strike is only a yellow flash in the sunlight. Two fangs penetrate the main neck artery and pump deadly poison.

Aletta hasn't seen what happened. She let him lie. He will probably rise over a while and waddles on, she thinks. It's only when she hears his wheezing that she turns around and looks at him. Foam bubbles out of his mouth. He pulls in his breath like someone who snores heavily. She climbs down, turns him on his side. She sees the fang marks and the blood that streams down his neck. Panic-stricken she tries to stem the blood flow. It doesn't help. She runs to the wagon, grabs a piece of cloth, and tries with it to no avail. She tries to lift his upper body but he is too lithe and heavy.

She sits next to him and starts to cry desperately. She sees how the liquor and poison cause spasms and the foam that increasingly comes out of his mouth. She sees how the wet spot grows on the dry sand.

She sees him die slowly right in front of her eyes.

Shock freezes her. Goosebumps over her whole body. Desperately she looks around but there is no one who can help her. Only nature around her. Quiet and tranquil. For a long time, she only sits indecisively and cries.

Eventually, she realizes she will have to do something. She tries to get her thoughts together, but it is too much for her mood.

Her father must be buried! She looks around. Where? It's only rocks and hard soil. Slowly she walks to the wagon, gets an old spade, and stands undecided. Near the trees, the ground looks softer. Through the tears that run like rivers, she slowly with a heavy heart treads to the trees. She nearly falls over the heap before she sees it. An old aardvark hole under the first tree. It will be much easier to open up this hole than to try and dig a new one.

The ground is even looser than she anticipated, more gravelly than solid. She shovels the hole that goes down with an angle. All sweaty and with dirty tear lines over her cheeks she slowly opens the hole. Her arms pain and her thin clothes cling to her wet, sweaty body.

Eventually, she is satisfied. But how is she going to get the body to the hole? She can't carry him. Maybe she can drag him along but she knows she will not succeed.

A donkey's bray nearby gives the answer. She gets a long throng and catches the tamest donkey. She binds the thong around its neck and the other end around her father's feet. Then she leads the donkey in the direction of the grave. She tries not to think about the damage grasses, shrubs and stones will do to his body. She simply must get him in the grave. She stops alongside the grave and unloosens his feet. The most whimsical part lies ahead. She rolls him into the grave. Luckily he falls face down. She covers the hole quickly.

She fastens the donkey to the wagon. Then she tries to get the other together. Two of them run away. She leaves them. Lion Head comes back from roaming the vicinity. He sniffs at the heap of ground and looks up to her. She strokes his massive head.

Half an hour later she is ready. The most essential things she packs onto the two donkeys. The one lighter because she might have to ride on him. She ties the bridles together so that she can lead them if necessary. Her father's tools she leaves in the wagon. She can do nothing with it. She uses a little water to wash her face and hands. Luckily, the river is nearby if she needs water.

The solemn procession starts to move. She walks in front leading the donkeys. On their backs are only a few, scant possessions.

A few pots, some clothes, meal, and dried meat, biscuits, and the rest of the guinea fowl. She travels parallel with the river. She is on her way to New Rush, where else? Somewhere ahead she will have to cross the river. Maybe somewhere there is a drift making it easy to cross. Lion Head follows leisurely.

"Goodbye, Dad!" she says bitterly. *Mother, I didn't leave him*. She cries without tears coming from her eyes.

When dusk falls, she makes camp. She binds the donkeys to the nearest tree. They start to graze the sparse grass under the tree.

It is quite dark when she has her meal ready. She knows she must eat, but the food thickens in her mouth. She has no tears left. She is afraid. If there is something like a Dear God, he'll have to help tonight. After her meal, she pulls a blanket over her and lies down next to the fire. Sleep mercifully wipes out the horror and hardships of the day.

The moon has already made a long way across the sky, when she awakes.

The donkeys. First, she hears them braying frightened. Then she hears the vicious growl of a leopard. Lion Head rushes forward and attacks the leopard. A few ferocious attacks from his side, then she hears his shrill yank, and then it is silent. In the dim light, she can see the one donkey turn his behind and kicks at the leopard. The other donkey comes loose and runs away and she can hear his galloping. She dimly sees the cat figure following that donkey.

Then it is silent. She turns, pulls the blanket over her head, and waits for the attack from some or other predator.

Tonight is my last night on earth, she thinks extremely terrified.

Chapter 6: The cancan girls

Rosa is standing in her hotel room in Cape Town and looks through the window down on a small square. While the girls are resting, she now has a little time to reminisce. Now that she has seen them, she wonders whether she is doing the right thing. Will they adapt? Will they fit in?

"Look," the owner of the hotel in New Rush told her. "It is becoming a crisis. The guys have too little to keep them busy. Now they waste their time by getting drunk, gamble, fight and breaking the hotel down. We must get girls!"

"Girls?" she asked.

"Girls. Dancers. Entertainers, whatever that can entertain the guys."

But in his eyes she saw his greed for money. Girls would attract more delvers to the hotel who would spend more and fills his pocket. But she agreed. There was no entertainment and girls on the diggings were scarce. Earlier she and Rosina, an Italian girl, held a dance show once a week, but since Rosina has run away with a farm boy, she was left alone and the shows stopped.

He looked at her questioningly as if she could solve the problem easily. And she did.

"I will get four girls from France. But it will cost you."

His eyes twinkled. "Four Frenchies! I shall pay!"

She wrote to her sister in Brussels. I'm looking for four girls, beautiful and well built, who can dance, but that is not so important. They must know something about the world and know men. Even if you take them off the street, I don't mind. We both were there. But they must be stunning and sexy, you understand what I mean?

And this morning they have arrived by ship. Pale Europeans, but beautiful and attractive. Angelique, a fiery French girl built like a goddess and outspoken. She is a bit bigger than the other three. Immediately started to moan about the bad food on the ship. Anita, the quiet one, a beautiful girl, dark like the Mediterraneans, slim and gracious with dark eyes. Sophie, also a handsome girl, a little plump but very easy to talk with. It is Michelle that immediately stole her heart. Blonde and beautiful, with a blushing countenance and endearing smile. She might look like a softie, but you soon realize this girl had to fight from her childhood for everything. Her enthusiasm for the future in Africa was heart-warming for Rosa.

Down in the square, a few boys are now kicking a ball around.

Yes, so life kicks you around before you know it. Before you know it, you are thrown out on the street and have to survive by the lust of men. That is why she fled, years ago, and together with musicians, worked her passages to the Cape. She heard about the diamond diggings and went inland by coach. There she got a job as a dancer and waitress. And for that, she pays whenever he chooses for his desires.

But it is alright. She doesn't need to sell her body on street. And in a way, Cohen is not repulsive to her. On the contrary, she likes him. His wife died years ago.

She smiles. They won't know these girls are not Frenchies but from Belgium.

"Girls," she says when they gather in the lounge after supper. "Early to bed. The following days are not going to be a joke. We will be travelling by coach for hundreds of miles. It is warm and dry inland. Take care of your skins. I've got enough cream."

Angelique strips immediately and grumbles something about treating them like babies.

"Listen, Angelique. I'm the boss. Another word from you … The ship is still in the harbour. Maybe you don't understand. I'm not dependent on you, you should be on me!"

Angelique pales frightened. Rosa with her soft, white skin, her round and friendly face did not look to her someone that can be frim.

"And this goes for all of you. The first time you give me any trouble, I'll kick you out even if it is in the middle of the Karoo."

She sees the question marks on their faces. "The Karroo is an enormous, flat piece of land we must pass to get to New Rush. It is dry and the sun bakes mercilessly. One day and you are gone forever."

Then she continues in a hard tone: "Do you understand me?"

Speechless they all nod. They have no idea what the Karoo is but they understand what Rosa says. And they are a little afraid also.

Anita wanted to ask whether they could walk around the city before bed, but now she keeps quiet. She wants neither to go back on ship that makes you seasick nor to be kicked out in a sort of hellish desert to be burnt to death like in hell.

Rosa is satisfied that her authority is established.

"Okay, let's go for a little walk. Then we return early and hit the sacks. The coach departs at four-o'-clock tomorrow morning."

Rosa feels pity for them. Only yesterday they have arrived after a long sea trip and tomorrow on their way. And nine to ten days of hell lie ahead before they reach New Rush. But it is better this way.

The sooner the worst gets past the better.

Chapter 7: The story of New Rush

"We must keep west until we reach a road to New Rush."

Chris measures the height of the sun. Maybe twelve-o'-clock. The sun is directly above them and tortures everything that is not under some shade of a tree. And many trees there are not on these bare prairies. Chris is in a hurry. He wants to reach New Rush as soon as possible.

Along the road Herklaas whined.

"What if he follows us? What if he comes and whips us with the sjambok?"

Chris wanted to say something but Samuel, irritated because he carries the heaviest sack, blurted out: "If you want to crawl back like a sick dog, turn around and fuck off before the path is overgrown with thorns."

Chris has more sympathy with his smaller brother: "He wouldn't know in which direction to look for us. If he starts to seek us he will probably go in Colesburg's direction. But let's take a rest under that thorn trees. And we taste how is his dried meat."

Samuel laughs: "Yes his biltong. And his bread. And his biscuits."

"And also the honey I have pinched. He likes it so much!"

When they sit down in the shade and start to eat they heckle further.

"Wonder whether he and Ragie had a peaceful nap."

"How much did you give her?"

"Almost nothing. The poor soul thought it was a fortune."

"And how much did you take?," asks Herklaas.

"Only a few pounds. He won't even miss it."

"It is theft," Herklaas remarks chewing on a salty piece of biltong.

"It's payment for all the free work we had done for him."

He is silent about his mother's jewels he took from a drawer in the bedroom.

"I wonder who milked the cows?" Samuel smiles.

"Himself. Who else?" laughs Chris, "Just imagine; he sits with hit fat stomach on a stool milking. I'm sure his stomach will prevent him to reach the teats."

"And even when he reaches it, I swear he will plash his pants sopping wet." Herklaas joins in. Samuel's words earlier did him a world of good. Forwards. No turning back.

"Or just say," Chris now is splitting his sides, "he touches Liesbek's sore teat and she kicks him from the stool so that he ploughs through the wet dung!"

"Or she hits him through the face with her wet pissed tail." Herklaas.

They simply enjoy these comic scenarios.

"And where will he look for the sheep tomorrow? He won't know whether they are at the fountain or behind the mountain. Give me another piece of biltong, Chris." Samuel.

Chris scrutinizes the horizon. He is looking for smoke somewhere but the air is only trembling with heatwaves. No sign of a homestead nearby. They will have to get water somewhere. In the veld are many furrows that are supposed to be fountains, but they are all dry now. He knows when they grow deep enough in the sand they might get some muddy water. For now, they are okay.

They lie down in the hot sand under the meagre shade to take a nap. If the flies only will let them.

It is Herklaas who awakens first an hour later. He gets a fright and anxiety clamps his stomach and his heart rushes. Unmistakably a gunshot in the silent afternoon air. It must be their stepdad who has caught up with them, he thinks pale in the face. And he is shooting at us!

"Chris! Samuel!" He nearly can't get out the hysterical sounds.

They awaken. Peeps around dazed. See nothing amiss.

Chris is red in the face.

"Why are you making so much noise? What is fucking wrong with you?"

Samuel puts his hand up. Another shot sounds.

"Someone is shooting somewhere. This is good news."

"Are you fucked in your head?" yells Herklaas. "What if it is dad!"

"Shut up!" Chris's voice is hard and stern.

Then they hear another crack.

Chris and Samuel smile. They know what it is. It is the cracking of a long whip that shatters the afternoon silence to pieces.

"Oh, g..goodnesss …" Herklaas stutters and looks around frightened.

"Come, we must make haste. Let's see if we can get to him. It sounds just beyond that hillock over there." Samuel has already picked up his things and starts to walk. Chris is a bit slower. Herklaas is still standing frozen.

"We can't …" he starts but then his throat contracts out of fear. Chris realizes he should clear up the misunderstanding.

"It is not a gun, silly. It is a long whip. And it is just in front of us. Probably a wagon on its way to New Rush."

Floods of relief wash down over Herklaas. He has told himself so many times not to be afraid, but every time something awkward happens he wants to wet his pants. He doesn't know why this is, but he wishes it was not like this.

They now walk hastily through the trembling afternoon air. The cracks become louder.

"He is moving to the right," Chris declares. "We must keep right of this hillock. I'm sure we'll get him further on."

 Samuel is quiet. His strong legs give giant strides and he leaves the other two behind. They must jog to keep up with him.

"Easy now, Samuel," is Chris wheezing behind him. "You walk as if you have got red ants in your pants. Come on, Herklaas. We are not going to wait for you. Samuel, slow down for fuck's sake."

"We must get to him. We don't know exactly where New Rush is. And I am now too damn bushed to walk further in this damn sun."

Chris knows it won't help to argue with Samuel. It is Samuel. He doesn't know the end of his strength. When he gets something in his head, you don't stop him. It is not every man who can take a young, fierce afrikaner bull by the horns and break his neck.

Chris was correct. Rounding the hillock they see the ox-wagon with sixteen red oxen in front of it moving to the right about 300 yards from them. On the wagon chest at the front of the wagon, the driver sits with a long whip in his hands which he cracks lustily and which sounds like gunshots over the oxen. In the meantime, he talks with his span of oxen because the earth is sandy and the heavy weight could sink the wagon into the sand up to the axles. That would be disastrous. Also, the wagon must keep moving. The ox-leader boy just in front of the sharp horns of the front oxen must listen carefully when the driver, after judging the earth's condition, orders him to lead the oxen somewhat left or right.

He sees the three boys coming from his right trying to catch up to the wagon. He himself would like to pee. He brings the procession to a stillstand on a gravelly little plateau. He climbs down and does his thing, sees how his water vanishes into the arid ground. It is a dry year and the sun is no one's mate. He takes off his wide brim hat and wipes the sweat from his forehead with the backside of his hand. From afar he forms an opinion of the three. The leader boy comes from the front. He orders him to make a little fire for coffee. The boy thankfully starts immediately.

Not many possessions with them. Each only carrying a rucksack. Also not smart clothes but old and worn. Surely poor boys on their way to New Rush. Okay, many are streaming to the diamond fields. Farm boys, foreigners, brown and black people. All with the glitter of diamonds in their eyes. He will look them through.

"Good day," he greets over a distance. He is a short, corpulent man, with a wide chest and a round face. His short hair clings to his superwhite forehead. Where the white of his forehead ends, the sun has tanned him brown. "Where are you going?"

"Afternoon, Uncle," greets Chris. He approaches the man with an outstretched hand. "I am Chris Strydom." The hand that grips his is smallish but clamps like a vice.

"Kobus Grundling," he greets while he literally crushes Chris's hand. "Pleased to meet you, Chris."

Herklaas also comes nearer. After he has endured the hand crush he wonders whether he would be able to write with his hand again. He could swear no bone is left unbroken.

Kobus smiles inside. He always enjoys the handshakes immensely. He knows he has a formidable handgrip. He enjoys it when he sees the pain in his opponent's eyes. And if he dislikes a person he clamps his hand until tears appear in his eyes.

He assesses Samuel. This is a mighty guy. Wait, let's see. Many big guys are really weaklings. However, when Samuel's hand clamps around his, he knows this is another class of man. Samuel's big hand folds around his smaller hand and the grip is firm.

"How do you do, Samuel," he smiles at Samuel and presses a little harder.

"Good afternoon, Uncle," Samuel greets back and timidly wants to undo his grip, but Kobus holds his hand and presses even harder. Samuel's hand is so much bigger than his that he can't get a solid grip.

"Well, boys. It's very nice to see you. For many miles, I haven't seen life." He now shakes Samuel's hand in the hope to get a firmer grasp. And then he presses with all his might.

Samuel is flabbergasted. He tries to loosen his hand but he feels the vice only pinch harder. He doesn't understand it. Why does this man not let his hand go? Then he feels the pain in his hand as the bones are pressed together and gradually he begins to understand. He knows he will have to do something quickly to get away from this painful grip. He looks around to Chris and Herklaas, but Herklaas' only worry is his own pain and he is not aware of the spell of strength playing it out in front of him. Chris's eyes are elsewhere. He tries to make out what is under the canvas which cover the cargo on the wagon.

Slowly but surely Samuel gets annoyed. He feels the crushing continues and the pain intensifies. He must concentrate not to let anything show on his face.

"On your way to New Rush?" Kobus asks and eyes Chris for a moment.

"Yes, Uncle," says Chris.

Kobus looks at Samuel. He looks him right in the eyes. He wants to see the expression of pain there. Then he will loosen his grip satisfied. But that is not what he sees. A wildness appears in the green eyes, they widen markedly, a frown jumps on his forehead and then he feels how the grip in Samuel's hand tightens, how the fingers become steel clamps and how they slowly clamp all tighter. Somehow the boy's strength will be spent, will he be over his peak. He tries to grip even harder but then realizes that he has reached his peak and not Samuel. He has underestimated this big guy.

He hears bones in his hand begin to crack. He has lost, he knows it. For the first time in his life, he has lost.

"Let's go and make coffee," he says quickly and takes Samuel's arm with his left hand. "Before you break my hand completely."

Samuel let go of his hand as if it is a hairy spider. Kobus rubs his painful hand. Goodness, this guy is immensely strong!

Later they sit around the fire each with a cup of coffee. The trio is really thankful for this luxury. For the last two days, they had only water to drink. When they approached homesteads they only asked for water, nothing else.

"And so you are on your way to the diamonds?" Kobus sips his very hot coffee, while his thoughts are on another track.

Chris instantly is excited. "Yes, Uncle. My brothers and I want to have a look and maybe get some work there. Do you think …"

"Oh yes. Plenty of work," he says with a twinkle in his eyes, "even if it is to carry the night buckets and piss pots to and fro. But wait, you will see for yourself tomorrow."

"Uncle, you say you are doing transport."

Kobus holds up his hand. "Listen you guys. Stop this 'uncle' business. I'm not that old and my name is Kobus." He doesn't wait for an answer because he is suddenly in a hurry to be alone and to think things through. "Yes, I'm a transporter. This load is corrugated iron for a house. I've got another two wagons on the way but they are heavier with all types of machinery on them from England. They are trekking slower. Will probably be at New Rush the day or so after tomorrow." He suddenly burst out laughing: "There was an Italian who wanted to pay me a lot of money to get a ride with me, but for his crow face I had no appetite. He will now come with the last wagon. He will learn Africa is not for sissies."

He sees the questions in their eyes want to bubble out of their mouths. He throws the last drops of coffee out of his cup.

"But now I must trek. You can walk with the wagon or if we are too slow you can follow the wagon's path ahead."

They start to move, the leader boy nimbly in front of the horns of the oxen, Kobus on the wagon chest with his whip that he swipes over the oxen and which he let crack like thunder, the trio behind the wagon in the wagon's spoors and over the sparse growth of grasses between the spoors.

Chris is fed-up. He wanted to ask so many questions. How does the town look, how big is it, how many people are there, how many diamonds are really delved, are there people who get stinking rich in one day, and what have you. He wanted to know whether the story is true of a man nearby who plastered his hut with mud and when the mud dried, the diamonds twinkled in the plaster. He wanted to know so much more so that he can begin to put the basis of a plan together.

It seems that Kobus deliberately wants to avoid their questions. Samuel likes Kobus. He likes strong men. After he was perplexed and realized it was a handgrip competition, exhilaration ran through him. Power against power and he has never experienced anyone who could hold the candle to him. He could read the admiration in Kobus' eyes. He smiles satisfied.

Herklaas is trotting along looking at the ground. He knows he is relieved it wasn't their stepdad who caught up with them but the road ahead seems very narrow. He is afraid of what lies ahead. He longs for his books that he had to leave behind. A few that had been his mother's, one that the teacher of the farm school gave him because he read so well and studied so hard. He was his standard far ahead. He longs for the secure protection of the classroom and his lady teacher. It was a safe haven, a friendly half-dark room with its few desks and handmade blackboard. Even his corner in the bedroom he had to share with his brothers, he longs for that. Sometimes he could hide there with his books. He wanted to bring the books along but Chris put his foot down. It is heavy and has no use.

Kobus' eyes roam the blonde plains in the blistering afternoon sun. They are doing fine. He could be in New Rush about noon tomorrow.

Tomorrow is the middle of the week and he has much to complete before Friday. His other wagons could be there and must be unloaded. Then he will pocket some money and buy more oxen. He must expand his transport business. New Rush is becoming a big town and the opportunities are many. Water, firewood, groceries are small change. Buildings, heavy machinery. That is where big money is to be made. He smiles when he remembers Gieljam Roos. His lopsided wagon broke in two halfway up Bruintjies Heights under the heavy weight. One side gave way and all the sheets of corrugated iron slipped down the decline. The wagon's single shaft broke off and the oxen, suddenly relieved from the burden behind them, lustily took flight uphill and only stopped at the top. It was of no use that Gieljam with his big voice swore them all to hell. That wagon will never be used again. He will simply have to wait until Kobus's new span and wagon arrives there. There is no other plan. And from his payment, he will have about nothing left.

Thus, there is a whole lot to do before Friday.

Then his brain tackles the thing for which he wanted to be alone. The arm-wrestling match on Friday evening. The thing has nagged the back of his mind from the moment Samuel crushed his hand. Except if another Goliath has arrived in New Rush in the meantime, there is no other man that can push his hand down and burn it on the candle flame. And the betting is going to be heavy, he knows. The guys have almost nothing to do over weekends as to sit and drink themselves drunk and the strongest guys frequently become involved in fights while the other then gamble on and win or lose their hard-earned money. And he needs money for the expansion of his transport business. Lots of money.

Cohen declared a big arm-wrestling match in the hotel and the winner can be sure of a pocket full of money. He simply must win the contest.

But now Samuel has come into the picture. And if he decides to enter the competition it could end up badly for himself. He doesn't at this stage know how to solve the problem. For a long time, he sits deep in thought, the whip idle in his hands.

When the sun moves tired in behind thin, fleecy clouds, he calls for a stop. He will have to lose the match flashes through his brain when the trio joins him and he again sees Samuel's formidable, muscular arms.

Then a brilliant brainwave hits him. He smiles broadly.

Jovially he talks to them. "Okay, boys. Let's sleep over here. Here is some water in a streamlet for the oxen and enough firewood to chase away predators. Tomorrow you will see the diamond city. Not much of a city; and the Colesburg Kopje is gone already."

"The Colesburg Kopje?" Herklaas is amazed.

Kobus looks at the trio. Raw farm boys. Are they going to fit in? Maybe some titbits for them.

"Okay, tell you what. Let us prepare ourselves for the night ahead. We'll make a fire and make supper. Then I will tell you the story of the Colesburg kopje"

Later they sit around the fire. Kobus puts a stick in the fire and lits his pipe. The smoke drifts away in a light breeze.

"Look, New Rush isn't the only diamond mine. There are Bultfontein, Dutoitspan, and salso De Beers. You will come to know them, but the story of New Rush really starts with De Beers. The guys who dug there weren't very satisfied with their profits and groups of them prospected elsewhere. Fleetwood Rawstone also prospected in the vicinity. He was not alone, his gang was called the Red Cap Party because of the red caps they wore. One evening they were out-camped near a hill then known as Gilfillan's Kopje, I don't know why."

His pipe has died down and he puts another stick in the fire and watches it burning before he lits his pipe.

"Well, Rawstone had brown chef from the Cape, named Damon. But Damon had one great weakness. It was Cape Smoke, a cheap but very strong brandy. And when he was pissed he became unruly and irritated Rawstone to no end. Annoyed Rawstone one evening banned Damon from the camp with food and utensils with the order to go and seek diamonds at the Kopje. I think he had hoped to get rid of Damon for good."

"But where does Colesburg Kopje fits in?" Chris asks. Kobus holds up his hand.

"I'll tell you just now. Two or three evenings later while Rawstone and his mates were playing cards, Damon burst into the tent. When he opened his hand, two or three smallish diamonds were in his palm. The gang immediately went to the kopje where Damon had dug and found diamonds. The next day they pegged their claims. Rawstone who was raised in Colesburg, then renamed it to Colesburg Kopje. That was in July last year. The news travelled like a veld fire and within a month there were two to three thousand diamond diggers."

He taps the ashes out his pipe against his boot.

"And there you have the story of the origin of New Rush. Tomorrow you will see it."

Chapter 8: Drama in Canada

Caprini feels like vomiting. The ship rolls in the waves. When last had he the nauseating feeling on his stomach, he wonders. Maybe the day when the Greek wanted to buy their claim because he was executing a life-threatening swindle.

He relives those moments.

Only when he realized the Greek really wanted to purchase their claim, the relief washed over him. The Greek held his hand up as if he waited for applause.

"Have you heard?" he bellowed again. "They are going to sell their claim to me!" Suddenly there was thunderous applause. If there wasn't any fight of a kind, this was enjoyable action of another kind.

"I don't think the claim is for sale," started Caprini carefully. Now he had to play his cards good and solid. He anticipated that they would get offers, but this is like lightning from the sky. He only hopes the lighting wasn't going to strike him.

"No, my man, the claim is up for sale. Everything on earth has a price, not so?" The Greek took a few swigs. The whiskey dripped from the corners of his mouth.

The guys cheer him on loudly.

"Now why would we … " Mac chipped in angrily but Caprini's voice drowned his. He had to handle this thing correctly. He didn't like a battered face, especially not his own. He talked loudly.

"You all know we struck it rich. You know we have the best claim along the whole river. You know we can't just sell it cheap."

Yes! Yes! The delvers yelled in a choir.

"So, if we are going to sell, the price will be high. There are heaps of gold. It is worth a lot."

The guys now were rowdy. It was just as good as a fistfight, this fight with words.

The Greek waved his hands. The guys settled down.

"He may be expensive, but I buy him." His voice was softer but firm. His earnest face and eyes said: if you don't listen, I will hit you until you understand. He took out a pouch of gold from his inner pocket, hopped it in his hand, and slammed it down on the counter.

"A fortune in that pouch, I tell you. It is enough for your claim."

Caprini picked up the pouch, weighed it carefully in his hand. It was a fortune. He swallowed deeply.

"It is not much more than we've got out in one afternoon," he said softly. He carefully looked at the Greek's eyes. "Sir, you will excuse me when I say this. It isn't enough." He tried to be as mild as possible.

The Greek was silent for a long time. Tension gripped the other men. They have seen more than once how the Greek broke someone's jaw with only one jab. The Greek's hands clamped open and close like dragon's claws. His eyes became slits. Caprini is on the point to capitulate when the Greek burst out laughing.

"My, but you are a good businessman," he bellowed, took another pouch out of his pocket, and handed it over to Caprini. "We write."

The barman handed over pen and paper. They wrote and signed.

"This round on me, guys!" he shouted happily. The men cheered and drank.

A half-an-hour later Caprini and Mac departed clandestinely with all their belongings on two mules upstream.

From there on it was easy. They bought useless claims, doctored them, and sold it for huge sums. Then they vanished during the night. When the guys discovered their treachery, they were long gone.

It was a dangerous game. There was little legal control in the area. Digger's law was the order of the day. If they caught you they hung you from the nearest tree or just shot you down and left you for the bears to devour. Nine months later, Caprini knew it was time to leave the country.

"Listen, since my childhood I had bad lungs. I can't stay in this cold and wet world any longer. I read they were discovering diamonds deep in the south of Africa. A few guys have already left to go there. We've got enough money. Are you going with me?"

Mac didn't like the idea. It was fun to make so much money. He enjoyed fooling the diggers. Moreover, the canteen owner told him that someone was interested in their newest claim.

"But it is dangerous. What if the Greek or someone else finds us here? I know we are hundreds of miles from them, but I have a feeling …"

"Let's make a last big killing and then we can go down to the coast on our way to the Cape"

Mac was hesitant for days until he imagined he saw one of the Greek's men in a canteen. Then he agreed. Fear suddenly gripped him so much so that he was eager to get away and offered to go ahead with the mules. Caprini should only give him his part of the profits if anything maybe went wrong. Caprini concurred and gave him only a part of his deal. They studied a rough map that they could find. They listened to the trappers who knew the country and promised each other to meet at the harbour. Caprini would sell the claim the next morning and follow him.

The Greek grinned when he saw him.

"Ah, mister Caprini, I hear you want to sell a claim!"

He drank out of a bottle. There was no one else in the canteen except one worker of the Greek.

Caprini turned around to run away, but the worker blocked the way by moving into the door opening, pulled out a sharp knife, and let his fingers caress the sharp blade.

"Oh no, mister Caprini, don't be in a hurry! We haven't discussed business yet. Let's have a drink." He poured his glass full of whisky and points to a chair at the opposite of a table.

Caprini sat down. His brain that had ceased to function suddenly feverously started to gallop. Many possibilities flashed through his head, but none of the explanations seemed to get him out of trouble. He was only thankful that his money and gold was well hidden before he came to the canteen.

"Where is that fucking Irishman?" the Greek asked vilely.

Caprini was in a dilemma. He couldn't tell the truth but it suddenly gave him an escape route. Keep calm, Caprini, he said to himself.

"That damn Irishman! That fucking, shrewd MacDonald. He is gone with all my money and gold. He just disappeared. I've got nothing. The mules, everything. I've got nothing. Only the claim to sell."

He looked like bursting into in tears. The Greek was silent. This was unexpected. He only looked at him with a question on his face.

"You won't understand but it is the Irishman's work. It is he that make the plans. He chooses the claims. I just had to do the dirty work selling it. I must do the talking and when someone wants to batter someone, they batter me. Look, there at …"

"Shut your fucking trap." The Greek had no inclination to listen to the sob story but when he looked at the pathetic, crying Italian, some pity filled him. Furthermore, it's not satisfactory to hit such a feeble man.

"Stop it!" He never could endure a crying man. "Bind him. Which way did MacDonald go?"

"I don't know. Maybe upstream. Where else. He left me here without …"

"Shut up! Bind him up thoroughly, Carlos. Take him to the barn. Then we go and look for Mac. If I lay my hands on him I will cut his throat."

Carlos grinned. He had seen when Mac departed. And he knew that night blood would wash over the sharp blade of his knife.

Caprini jumped around as well as he could. His hands and feet were tied but with immense effort, he could eventually stand upright. Then he jumped like a frog and yelled. The mules became anxious and brayed loudly but it was only late that afternoon that the caretaker came and freed him. He bought two mules and in a great hurry followed the route he knew Mac and his followers had taken. He was unsure whether they believed his story. He rode on one mule. It was almost dark. Frequently he stopped and tried to listen to sounds. He was afraid.

Later on, it became dark and the mules got frightened by birds flying up. He decided to stop for the night. In a little open patch next to the path, he bound the mules tightly and got some twigs to make a fire. Then he heard the sound of hoofs. He crawled nearer to the path and tried his best to see in the dark. The sounds came from the front and the riders were in a hurry. His heart nearly stopped when they passed him. The Greek and Carlos mercilessly hit the mules.

Early the next morning, he followed the path. His mind was in a turmoil, his intestines in a knot. He went on for miles, he can't remember exactly how many, because of the misty rain. Then across the path he saw the drags and fight marks. He followed it slowly and anxiously until he saw Mac's boots protruding from under a bush. Then already he knew, but cautiously he went nearer and pushed the branches aside. Mac was on his back, his lifeless eyes staring up in the sky, his throat a gaping wound, the blood a dark red patch under his neck. Caprini vomited.

He didn't even take time to look for Mac's gold or money. The Greek wouldn't have left without it. He didn' even close Mac's eyes. He was afraid of the reproach in them. He fled. For days he relentlessly drove the mules until a river stopped his flight. Then he bribed Red Indians to row him downstream to the coast.

The ship rolls forward and sideways simultaneously. Just in time, he grabs into a bundle of throngs. A wave bursts over the deck and hits him. He tastes the salt and it burns in his eyes.

Dammit, he thinks, if I survive this voyage, I will never set my foot on a ship again.

Chapter 9: Staanvas

She awakes when the first light creeps over the horizon.

He is sitting on his haunches. Motionless like a statue. She sees him immediately silhouetted against the rosy background of the rising sun. She is frightened.

He stands up slowly and comes nearer when he sees she has awakened. Her heart thunders in her chest.

"Don't be frightened, Madam. It's me, Staanvas. I have been looking that no one might hurt you. I have been sitting here for hours."

She doesn't reply and only stares at him with big eyes.

"Staanvas has followed your tracks. Staanvas is not in a hurry. He walks slowly and rests frequently. That is why I hadn't met up with you. I saw the grave. You buried your husband nicely."

"My dad," she stutters.

"Your tata." He clicks with his tongue. "What?"

"A snake bit him."

He just shakes his head. Silly man to get yourself bitten by a snake.

"The leopards, they killed the dog and caught one donkey.

She only nods.

"I shall walk with you. I am also on my way to New Rush."

His eyes are asking. Does she have a choice?

"All right. I don't have much."

"That's okay. Staanvas also walks like that." He points his forefinger into the air.

She realizes he is waiting for her to say something. Then she makes a guess.

"Here is a little bit of leftover from last evening. There is guinea fowl."

She sees how his face lights up. "If you make a little fire, we can make witgat root for coffee. It's all I've got."

He is highly elated. Hunger has been gnawing for days, but he is too injured to kill hares or dig for roots to eat. He survived by eating grass and berries for many days. Since that day the big Kora brothers caught him and hit him with fists and knobkieries. It was all the result of his attention to a girl with the most beautiful buttocks in the country.

He devours the rest of the guinea fowl. He wants to leave her some scraps but she gestures he must finish it off. She chews on a piece of biltong and a biscuit. They drink their coffee out of two tin cups. She watches him carefully. Long, brown hair, light brown complexion with high cheekbones. Black, deep eyes that sometimes seem not to look at anything. A few hairs on his chin. She reckons he must be slightly older than herself, maybe a little older.

"Are you a Griqua?" She knows how proud the people of this ethnic group are.

He laughs while still chewing the last of the guinea fowl. A big, open mouth laugh.

"I'm a mixture of many things. My granddad was a Frenchman, so I am from the people from over the waters." He puts one finger in the air. "My grandmother was a Khoi, so I am from Africa." Another finger in the air. "My father married a Malay woman, the descendants of the slaves, so, I'm from the East as well." A third finger. "But my father chased me and my mother away. We then trekked with the herd farmers all along the west coast until my mother's death a few years ago. From then on I have walked my own way up to the great river, the Gariep, and all along the river visiting the Kora and Griqua settlements. But now I am going to the diamond fields."

She knows it is only a synopsis of a much bigger story. Staanvas is an interesting man.

"And your name? You can call me Aletta."

"Oh, my name. My real name is Stavast. It is French. But in our vernacular, they call me Staanvas. Stand fast."

After a while, they are on their way with him in front leading the donkey. She follows. When she becomes too tired, she will mount the donkey. He is walking very slowly.

"Have you been hurt?" she calls from the back. She notices sometimes he limps over rough terrain.

"A little."

She fingers through a little pouch and takes out a piece of root.

"For pain and fever," old Katryn said. "Just chew it well."

He takes the medicine gratefully. His body can't really do what he is doing. It feels as if some ribs are broken but he must help her. Such a beautiful girl, but not his taste. Too slender, her buttocks too small. But a beautiful face she has.

"We will get the road coming from the Cape somewhere to the front, but maybe tomorrow," she says.

He looks at the height of the sun with his black eyes.

"It will be tomorrow."

Chapter 10: Inland

It was far worse that they had anticipated.

The Cape was beautiful as they were travelling over green hills all through interesting towns and hamlets. Paarl and Wellington were beautiful little towns. Then they took the long stretch around the mountains through villages and farms to Ceres. Michell's Pass just before Ceres scared the hell out of them. More than once they drove on the edge of an abyss of which you can't see the bottom. It was hot. A dry west coast wind was blowing and the inside of the fancy Zeederberg Coach soon became an oven. It was one of the smaller coaches for carrying six people.

The dust of the hoofs of the horses forced them to keep the windows shut. Although most of their baggage were stashed on top, smaller items and handbags lay on the floor of the coach detrimental to leg space. Rosa sat on one of the seats and the other had to take turns to sit next to her. Opposite her three of them sat on the seat with little space between them. There, they had to take turns to sit in the middle. Angelique was the first to complain. First, she tried with an excuse because of headache not to sit in the middle but when Rosa ignored her, she grumpily stopped that and start to irritate the rest by shifting around. The bumpy ride in the coach was uncomfortable enough to make all edgy and her shifting around made it worse. Rosa had to raise her voice at times.

Moving from Ceres more inland they left the greener landscapes behind. I her mind's eye Rosa envisaged their route. Next town Sutherland. Then a long trek to Fraserburg. Thereafter miles to Victoria West and from there a murderous trek To New Rush. The terrain was now more flat than hilly. As they move more inland the vegetation changed from grasslands to flat, dull Karoo bushes and bushy hills as far as your eye can see. Even Michelle, who only sat staring wordless out of the window, could not hold it in.

"This is so different from Europe. Does it look like this in the whole of South Africa?"

Rosa didn't know what to say. She didn't know how the rest looks but she heard there were mountainous regions which are fascinating and along the east coast in Natal it was lush, green and beautiful. They also told her if the west gets enough rain the whole region looks like a garden with flowers. She herself liked the changing Karoo, from bushy areas to blonde grassy patches and she loved the smell of the bushes and shrubs after the rain.

After the cramped and cluttered existence in Brussels she liked the spacious plains and it was one of the things that extinguished the storm in her. Good and well to earn money with your body and then to play darling to one or other politician or rich guy who left you with a feeling that you are a cheap slut. There are prostitutes, street whores and sluts. There is a difference and she had still her pride and that is why she left.

"No. I heard there are beautiful parts as well," she answered eventually.

"I like it although it scares the hell out of me. Imagine you alone in this emptiness ..." Anita remarked, her long black hair tumbling over her shoulders.

Sophie just shook her head. "No, thank you. Not for me. I hate it. It is as if you ride into nothing without course and with no end. Rather give me the big city. At least I can say where I want to go."

They all smiled at her. It was true. This was a strange world.

Angelique could not get her disgust under control. "If it wasn't so damn hot. And if only I don't have to choke from dust. The nature has no effect on me. I feel nothing for it and nothing against it."

Rosa just sat and look them through silently. The outburst, the crisis would come, she knew it, but she already had a plan.

Today is the fourth day of their journey in this hellish sun. Although they stop every fifteen to twenty miles at one or other depot, it is just to change horses and this takes only minutes. Little time to thoroughly strecth your legs or lie down for just a minute to rest your tired body. The ride is bumpy and you are shaking and is thrown from side to side in the cabin even if you hold onto the strap installed for that purpose in front of you.

After the little longer stop in the afternoon for a change of horses, they all feel a little fresher. They could wet their faces with luke warm water and wash their hands. Shortly they are on their way again. And the Karoo is murdering them. It is only an half an hour later that Angelique's bad mood raises higher than the heat and she lets go at Michelle next to her.

"Michelle, you are sitting the place full like an obese Belgian whore!" She bumps into her.

Michelle at first is quiet, trying to shift away from her but then she bumps against Anita who is sitting at the window.

"Sorry, Angelique," she apologises to prohibit a confrontation, but Angelique's lid is off.

"The damn seat is too narrow with you and Anita's fat bodies ..."

Rosa sees how the blonde girl gets annoyed, how she presses her lips together, how her eyes are on fire. She holds up her hand before Michelle can utter a word.

"Stop the coach!" she yells at the driver through the hatch.

He holds in the horses and slowly they come to a stop. Angelique jumps out furious.

"Stay where you are," Rosa calmly instructs Michelle and Anita.

She rises and closes the door. She slides the window down. "If you can't control yourself and make it easy for us to travel with you, you can walk. Back to the Cape if you so wish or follow us, I don't care. I promised you …" She taps against the latch.

"Drive on!"

Flabbergasted Angelique sees how the coach starts to move and increasingly gather speed. Within a few seconds there is no way she can catch up, even if she runs. Okay, I will show them. She begins to walk back with the warm afternoon sun in her face.

The meerkat stops amazed nibbling his root. He had to jump out of the way of the horses and coach racing towards him where he sat in the spoor of the road. After the coach has passed him, he stood on his hind legs and looks to make sure the danger has passed. Then he again sits down and chews on his root.

The strange thing now coming towards him, he has never seen before. Unsure he sits upright and watches it approaching. His hole is half a yard in front of him next to the spoor. The thing comes closer but stops ten yards from him. They are looking at each other without moving. Then a sudden gust of wind moves the hair and dress of the thing. Maybe this thing is dangerous. With his formidable tail in the air he jumps forward on the spoor to get to his hole next to the spoor and vanish into it. He only hears the shrill yell of the thing and crawls deeper into his hole.

Rosa has stopped the coach a hundred yards further. They all climbed out. Looking at Angelique they see how she purposefully walks away from the coach. Then she stops. Moments later she yells, turn around and runs. When she arrives at the coach she is pale and wet of sweat. Shaken to her bones she tells them about the wild beast that wanted to attack her. Rosa doesn't say anything, only gets water out and gives them each a drink. Then she climbs back in the coach and the rest follows. Angelique sits whimpish and small in her corner.

The coach moves on. Rosa sighs. Many days of travel lie ahead.

Chapter 11: A hurtful dream

They are going forward slowly but she doesn't care. They have left the river and are now following vague spoors eastwards. With his knobkierie, Staanvas has managed to kill an unsuspected bunny. With her meagre amount of maize, she made meals for them. Sometimes Staanvas could manage to unearth a knoll with his kierie but she can see that he is badly injured.

He really doesn't bother her, she thinks. He is living in his own world, his eyes on the horizon as if he could get answers by looking at it. But she was very thankful that she is not alone. Two are better than one on these dry plains. Through the night, he manages to keep the fire burning to keep predators away, and when the jackals whine, she isn't so afraid anymore. She needs the time to work through her harrowing experience. To think about her mother, her father, and her future. What happened in the past, she in time has come to accept, she tempered her hatred and forgave her mother and father. "It is God's will" like her mother always said. Maybe she was right, maybe she was wrong. But it was the past, nothing can change it and it doesn't help to worry about it. The current situation is too bright around her. Staanvas and the donkey are nearer than her father, the stars that seem to come down and lie on you, nearer than her mother who she believes is in heaven just beyond the stars.

But it is the future that sometimes grips her heart. What will she do when they reach New Rush? Is it a place where she can find work even if it is to scrub floors and wash clothes and iron them. Where will she sleep? All the people she knows have some place to stay in, how poor they might be, even if it is a shelter made of branches like the Bushmen and many of the Kora next to the Gariep. If her mind only can get some grip on the situation in New Rush, it would help. Staanvas can't help her with that. He isn't thinking much about his future.

He only now and then sees the girl with the wonderful buttocks.

It was such a nice time there at the Bostanders. A wonderful clan of Khoi, more peaceful and placid than the other groups he encountered along the river.

They were not even reluctant to accept him as one of the clan because he had one advantage. He could fix wagons. He could fix wheels, make new spokes, cut a shaft, called a disselboom from a tree, make new yokes, and their neatly fitted pins called skeis. But what fascinated them the most was his ironwork, taking a red hot iron tyre, called a band, out of the fire, and fitted it over the wheel. All this he had learned in the Cape when his family was intact. Later on, he accompanied transport wagons to Algoa Bay. And after his father had chased them away, he helped to service the wagons of the trekking herd farmers.

Kolbooi Visagie, the leader of the clan Bostanders, liked him although he was generally against foreigners coming into his camp.

They looked well after him and allowed him to erect his own shelter of branches a little outside the clan's dwellings. They sent him food daily. Sundays he could join the men under the big tree and drink beer. The women then made food and serviced the men. He was satisfied.

Nikala was in early puberty. She was slender, big for her age, and sexually advanced. But it was her beautiful, round buttocks that enfired his hormones. From behind, her walk was fascinating! And she was attracted to him. From day one he realized that she clandestinely watched him. It was she who brought his food, who was watching him at work, who brought cold water when he sweated with spokes and the blistering sun tortured him. Then she came and stood very close to him, apparently in awe of his skill of handling his primitive tools so sufficiently; the way he could for hours carve a spoke or yoke, his skills to hit the iron with the hammer and the sparks that seemed to touch his body look as if it could inflame him.

Once in a while, their eyes met. Then she shyly looked away and ran off. During the hot nights, he couldn't sleep. When it became too hot in his shelter, he walked out in the cooler night air. Then he tried to see whether there was any movement in her fathers' hut. He wished she could come out and join him. For hours his body wouldn't leave his mind until he lied down tired of roaming in the early morning just to be awakened only a short while later by the yelling of children. It was because of her he stayed longer than he actually wanted because he was on his way to the diamond fields.

Because of her, he now moves with a body that yearns for rest that makes each step torture. But every day is a little better than the previous one. He could have been a corpse.

It was a lazy Sunday. Early the morning there was stuffiness in the air that made the lazy steps of the men even slower than usual. They came out of their huts sluggishly, looked up into the air, wiped the sweat from their foreheads, and thanked the forefathers for this day of respite. They went down on their haunches and took out their little snuff boxes and snuffed. Others took out their bone pipes, put tobacco in, and blew out blue smoke that lazily climbed into the air. They started to talk loudly about the rain they expected to come the next day although it was clouded and stuffy.

By noon they were well fed, well intoxicated, and very sleepy. One by one they sought the shade of a tree just to drop there and visit their forefathers. No lion would be able to roar them to life. The mothers and daughters sponged off their sweaty bodies and chose the coolest place in the huts to lie down with eyelids heavy. Only half an hour after the first snoring could be heard they were all in dreamland. The children vanished downriver to go and swim and gather bird's eggs. They knew they shouldn't bother the grown-ups for the whole afternoon. They would only return late in the afternoon.

 Staanvas had no inkling to go and sleep in his hell-warm shelter. Slowly he strolled down to the river, stripped, and swam in a lukewarm pool. Thereafter he stretched out on the lawn in the half-shade of a tree and only threw his pants over his bottom.

He must have slept a while and turned on his side with his face to the river. He dreamt. Nikala came out of the river stark naked. On her brown skin drops of water were glittering in the sunlight. She took her dress which she had thrown down carelessly before and pulled it over her wet body. Slowly she walked towards him her hips, swaying with each step, gracious like a young ibex. It is only when she bent over him and touched his shoulder that he realized it was no dream. Only when her cool body pressed against him that he knew his wildest dreams came true.

The next few hours were pure happiness and pleasure. It was dead quiet next to the river.

Her guardian's yell cut through the afternoon silence. She turned around and yelling on top of her voice ran to the huts.

Nikala shook him.

"Run! Get away! They are going to kill you!"

He knew what it meant. She hadn't been through the ritual allowing her to make love to a man. He got his clothes on hastily and ran upstream as hard as he could. Only later in the afternoon, her three brothers caught up with him. They hit him with their fists and knobkieries. He realized they were going to kill him. When he got a wee chance, he dashed out from under their torture and ran like never before in his life.

The female leopard was licking her cubs. She hid them under a tree in a secure bush nicely prepared for her cubs. There they could hide in safety deep in the thorn bush when she would be forced to go and hunt. She saw how the sun went down in the west and she knew soon she had to leave her lovies soon to go hunting. Her tail wagged and the three cubs made tiny outcries from pleasure when she licked them. Wonderful to be so cosy with mum. The next moment something bursts into the shelter and tried to hide.

When Staanvas rushed into her shelter so suddenly, she got a fright and she burst out like lightning and sprinted straight in the direction of the followers. They nearly pissed themselves wet from fright, turned around, and ran away yelling. Staanvas didn't wait to see how far the leopard chased them. He crawled out from under the bush and took to his heels as quickly as his injured body allowed.

For days he followed the river upstream. He avoided every settlement. He didn't want to leave a track. After some time he realized they didn't follow him anymore.

Days after that and after crossing the Gariep in a drift and following an arbituary of the river, he came across the tracks of the wagon. Slowly and with a sore body, he followed it.

He found the dilapidated wagon deserted. He was amazed. Footprints of the donkeys and that of a horse he could understand, but not the strange drag marks. When he saw the fresh heap of ground he began to understand. The corpse, he knew would be unearthed before the night is over and soon the scavenging vultures will have picked from the bones all the flesh the jackals and leopards left. He looked through the wagon, got hold of some tools, and slowly followed the tracks of the donkeys.

He is glad he came upon her. He is glad she doesn't ask too many questions. Tomorrow if they have luck, they will probably get the road from the Cape to New Rush, and then it would only be a few hour's walk to New Rush.

Chapter 12: Arrival

"And there you see it. This is how it looks."

Kobus climbs down and joins the trio next to the wagon. He laughs: "Looks quite miserable for a millionaire's dream!"

From a distance, they can make outbuildings; stone houses, corrugated iron buildings, wooden structures, and tents in long rows. Further on, Kobus explains, are the shacks and shelters of many workers seemingly disorderly. To their right, they can see scaffolding and material shining in the sunlight. They can see people, scurrying to and fro, some with wheelbarrows. To the left, they can see a mound of earth and also there it is no short of an ant nest. Wagons are all over the place with firewood, barrels of water, vegetables, and other necessities.

"It looks chaotic," Chris says, scratching his head. It is difficult to envisage what he really expected, something more like Colesburg and also Bloemfontein that he had visited once with his stepdad only to care for the horses and no more.

Kobus laughs out loudly. "Don't be fooled by this motley town. Here is quite an order. You will find that the diggers have their own laws, apart from the English that tries to maintain a strict order. Here is now a jail and the courts have been relocated from Klipdrift to New Rush." He points at a relatively new structure.

"Does this fall under the Cape Colony? Isn't it part of the Orange Free State?" Herklaas asks amazed. In school, they have learned that the Free State's border is further west.

Kobus laughs again. "Yes, it was until a few months back, in October if I remember correctly. First, they gave the diamond fields to the Griqua. Only a few days later it was simply taken over by Governor Barkly as English territory annexed to the Cape Colony. There will be a court case about this landgrab. I don't think President Brand of the Free State will give up easily. But at this stage, it is not officially part of the Cape Colony. The Cape parliament doesn't want to annex it. Much English politics behind it I don't understand well."

Herklaas wants to ask more questions but suddenly he stresses. Now that they are here, fear overwhelms him. His heart beats in his chest and his stomach turns.

"Where are we going to stay?" he communicates his fear.

"I have a corrugated iron store in which some of my workers overnight sometimes. You can stay there while you look for accommodation during the next few days. But now, my cargo must be unloaded."

"We'll help," Samuel offers. Kobus smiles. He has hoped they would help.

"Okay, let's go." He gestures to the leader boy to get going. The trio follows him.

A while later they are moving in between the first corrugated iron buildings. Herklaas follows reluctantly. He is tired and is in no mood for work. He hasn't thought much about his future but as he feels now, he is in no mood to stay in this place. Too much going on; too many people. A strange place. He is amazed when at the third building on their right he sees posters glued against the corrugated wall. Curiously he stops and starts to read. A notice of the arm-wrestling match Friday evening, another of a delver's meeting, another of information about claims. The door is open and curiously he peeps inside. It is half dark in the room but he can make out stacks of paper. Behind it, against the back wall, he sees a funny machine-like thing. He can't make it out clearly. A shellfish thing with a flat top.

He quickly peeps down the street to see where the wagon has gone. He just wants to finish reading.

When he looks back, a long sinewy man with a face resembling that of a camel, is standing in the door opening. He gets a fright and tries to open his mouth but words get stuck in his throat.

Jans Wildenboer is in a horrid mood. He moved here only a month ago and brought his printing outfit to New Rush. It cost heaps of money. He had this office built and with his letter setter start working. Soon he had enough work to keep him quite busy. One wanted a notice to put up at his claim, another to advertise for accommodation, the hotel wanted new menus, official proclamations from the magistrate, and what have you.

They worked from dusk to dawn. His letter setter, an intelligent Malay man, he brought with him from the Cape. He taught him and he did excellent work. This morning, however, he didn't turn up for work. When Jans enquired, people told him that the man has moved off to Bloemfontein. He didn't want to stay here any longer. He hankered too much to the mountains of the Cape, the wine, and the Cape girls. One can only shake one's head! He took his belongings and got a lift on a transport wagon. It left Jans in a terrible dilemma. He has got so much work.

He looks at the young man in front of him. He observes the shabby figure in front of him. Feeble yes, but he doesn't look too stupid. He pulls his eyes in slits.

"Can you read? Can you write? Are you looking for work?"

Herklaas frightens again and almost wet himself. He is unsure which question he should answer. He mutters only a vague 'yes' over his dry lips.

"Now, don't just stand there. Come inside so that I can explain what you have to do!" Herklaas stupidly steps into the office. Maybe he must turn around and run.

"Come on, don't be afraid. You seem to be a clever guy. Just what I need!"

Within a half an hour Herklaas is being promoted to a letter setter. It is not difficult and his spelling of Dutch and English is fine. Maybe he's got a feeling for letters and language, Jans prayed more than he thinks. And he works quite fast. Might it be that the young man does good work! He's got big plans. He wants to establish a formidable printing enterprise throughout South Africa. And maybe a Dutch newspaper. There are already two English newspapers on the diggings.

"My brothers ..." Herklaas soflly says.

"Oh, yes. I've nearly forgotten." He thinks for a moment. "I tell you what. I am staying behind the office but there is a small room next to it that my previous worker used. You can lodge there. Your brothers are with Kobus, not so?"

"Yes, and some of my stuff also."

"Of course. Tell you what. I must quickly go to the hotel with print work. I know where Kobus is. I will tell your brothers and bring your stuff. I dearly want you to finish this work before tonight. It is very important for our business."

Our business? Herklaas don't know whether his words are just to fool him but the words suddenly instill a feeling of importance. Maybe he is worth something.

"Thank you, Sir. I think I will be finished by evening." He points to the set board.

"Marvellous! I'm going now. I'll pick up something to eat as well."

As if he is afraid that Herklaas will leave everything and run away, he picks up the printed pamphlets and vanishes through the door. Outside, he suddenly stops in his tracks, put his head around the door opening.

"If you work hard, I shall pay you well." Then he's gone.

While he energetically commences with the work, he tries to make sense of the happenings of the last hour but his head is in a turmoil of conflicts. He's got a job, he is part of 'our business' and will be paid well. What if Wildeboer is dissatisfied with his work and what if he gets annoyed or what if he is only abusing him like their stepdad always did? What if this man chases him away like a bad dog? What if his worker comes back?

To get rid of all the negative thoughts he concentrates heavily on the letters. He was still very hard at work when Jans returns.

"Come out!" he calls from outside.

Herklaas quickly goes out. Then he hears it. The crack of a whip and galloping horses. The coach comes with quite a speed into town.

"What?" Herklaas is curious.

"The coach that brings the girls."

"What girls?"

"The cancan dancers from France for the hotel."

Herklaas wants to enquire further but he shuts his trap. Maybe he might sound like an utter fool.

"Let's walk down to the hotel. Maybe we can see something of the beautiful ladies. Close the door!"

Chapter 13: The dramatic entrance of the cancan dancers

After they have crossed the Riet River near New Rush, Rosa decides that they should rest for a while. She allows them to play in the shallow water, to bathe, and to cool off. According to the driver, it is only a few hours of travel ahead. She planned to arrive at New Rush late in the afternoon. Moreover, she wants to stop half an hour before they reach their destination to titivate themselves. It will not be delightful to go into town all weary and uncared for. She plans a grand entrance. She suddenly feels delighted that the trip is nearing its end. Luckily she had little trouble with Angelique but she can see that the irritation lies just under her skin. Therefore, she allows them to enjoy themselves. They are playing like jubilant children, splashes one another with water, and plays with their hands in the water.

Rosa watches them playing. Her sister's choices were not bad at all! They are beautiful young girls. She can see from their movements they are supple. She will easily teach them some dance steps and kickups. Angelique, especially, with her larger and busty physique should be an exquisite fiery dancer. The other three have moderate temperaments and her favourite, Michelle, is a dear child.

The language might be a problem, but not for long. They all speak French but also know a little Flemish. Michelle, being Flemish, can help them with Dutch or the vernacular the Boers speak here.

"You don't have to dress up now. We will stop later on and dress up and do our make- up. We are going to enter New Rush like princesses. Remember, they are waiting for weeks for your arrival."

Soon the coach is running happily along the dusty road. They near the place where Rosa plans to make a final stop.

Suddenly the driver holds in the horses. In front of him in the pathway is a strange procession that he doesn't understand. A limping man leading a donkey with a girl riding on it. He pulls in the reins so that the horses just trod along. He waits for the procession to move out of the way to pass them.

"There are people in front in our way," says Michelle leaning out of the window. "A girl on a donkey."

"Stop," Rosa orders the driver. "How long before New Rush?"

"Half an hour, more or less."

Rosa peeps through the window. This place is as good as any other.

"Get the coach there under the trees," she orders.

Staanvas tried to pull the donkey out of the track but it has its own mind. It is tired because it had to carry the girl for hours.

Staanvas turns around and watches the coach moving to the shade of the trees. He only gets the donkey half out of the way but Aletta doesn't dismount.

"Shame!" Michelle calls when she climbs down and sees Aletta. The shy eyes peeping from under her bonnet immediately arouses a motherly endearing in her. They all have now climbed down and silently are staring at Aletta and Staanvas.

"Come, girls! Let the people be. We have nothing to do with them." She turns to the driver. "Get the upper suitcases down. And bring water from the barrel."

"And what about her?" Michelle cannot turn her eyes away from Aletta.

"And what about her!" Rosa speaks harshly. "Come now, Michelle. Don't annoy me. It is a strange girl with her companion and their way to where ever. We have nothing to do with her!"

"But we can't leave her like this. See how she looks! She needs help!"

The driver, in the meantime, spoke a few words with Staanvas.

"A snake killed her father. He got her in the veld and is helping her to reach New Rush," he translates quickly.

Rosa is unsure. Again she looks at the girl. She is the same age as her girls, more or less, but woefully dressed. There are only a few earthly possessions on the donkey. Am I now doomed to be the guardian angel of poor, miserable girls? No! She shakes her head.

Aletta turns around and gestures to Staanvas to proceed. Slowly Staanvas starts moving. He wants badly to get rid of the girl. Arriving with her in New Rush might invoke questions. This land is not friendly to people of colour and the British are arch racists. He turns his head and talks to the driver. He translates.

"He asks you must take her along. She is bushed."

"Rosa, please. I ask a big favour."

Rosa sighs. If it were Angelique or one of the other girls, she would have declined, but Michelle …"

"Okay, then. Tell him the girl can stay but we can't help him."

Staanvas stops when he hears her words.

He turns around. "Go with them. It will be better …"

Aletta is quiet. She sits on the donkey until Michelle is next to her. She looks down in the friendly round face. Michelle speaks but she doesn't understand a word. Michelle suddenly remembers that the people here speak in a language that sounds like Flemish. It is a form of Dutch. Rosa uses it with some of the inhabitants. She knows Flemish and tries that. She tells her to climb down and go with her. Aletta is too tired to think about what the best option might be. Meekly she climbs down. Staanvas quickly takes off her belongings. It is nothing more than a little bag of utensils.

"I am keeping the donkey for now," he says quickly, afraid she might change her mind.

"Thank you, Staanvas. Keep the donkey." Tears well up in her eyes. Michelle leads her to where a bucket of water has already been placed for them to get rid of the dust.

The other girls greet her and curiously look at her from head to toe with disgust. She doesn't look dirty, only full of dust for she also has bathed and washed her hair in the river. But her dress is dirty and torn.

Michelle waits until all of them are finished. Then she pours more water into the bowl and washes herself. She turns to Aletta.

"Take off your bonnet," Rosa says. She is glad Michelle has taken responsibility in the meantime.

Aletta looks at Michelle questioningly. She gestures to the bonnet. Aletta unties the strings and removes her bonnet. A thick bush of brown hair tumbles down her shoulders. Unkempt but a beautiful bush of golden-brown hair. She is standing with her back to the girls and washes her face and thereafter wipes the rest of her body with a damp cloth under her loose-hanging dress.

In the meantime, Michelle talks to Rosa.

"We are the same size. I'm going to give her one of my dresses and a pair of shoes. I will titivate her."

Aletta turns around and sees the amazement on their faces. Without the bonnet and with a clean face it is a beautiful girl who faces the girls. Michelle is in seventh heaven.

"Een schone meid! Wonderful. Amazing!" She delves for the yellow dress and excitedly hands it over. Dress up, she signals but Aletta gestures to the driver and his helper. Rosa yells something and they vanish to the other side of the coach. Aletta takes off her torn dress and for a few moments is standing stark naked in front of them only with a panty. They gasp for breath. Perfectly built, like a French marble statue. Then she throws the yellow dress over her head. It fits perfectly. Michelle passes a hairbrush. Aletta brushes her hair. It is not successful. Michelle has a plan. She gets a yellow ribbon and gestures to Aletta to bind up her hair. It works. Suddenly everyone is smiling at her. She isn't the poor, unkempt girl on a donkey anymore, she is one of them. A beautiful girl with the body of a Greek goddess.

Rosa smiles. She gets the creams and makeup. The girls greedily reach for it. For so long they have been waiting for this day. To make up properly, to be scented with expensive French perfume and to experience the exhilaration of it and to imagine they are on their way to the Fontainebleau Castle.

Rosa winks for Aletta to join her. She now takes over. She is beautiful but hopelessly unkempt. The guys will fall over their feet for her. On the spot, Rosa decides. She must become one of her group. She will be a brilliant attraction. Over how exactly, she will worry later. She is sure when Cohen sees her, he will be excited. He will look at her and work out how much money he could make from her. The foul man! She suddenly intensively longs for him.

Cohen is standing in front of his hotel. He is dressed smartly in a tuxedo, white collar, and all. Curious bystanders join him. Over, at the other side of the road, the delvers have formed a dense row. They are standing around, joking, and jesting. They came from all over and are constantly joined by newcomers. Surely, no work is being done this afternoon. Some are talking loudly after having frequented some canteens. Noisily they all wait but then their noises are inundated by the sound of horses' hoofs.

"Here they come!" yells one loudly. The others join in yelling and screaming.

The coach enters the market square and with a wide, fancy turn stops right in front of Cohen.

Cohen waits until the dust has settled and driven away on the afternoon breeze. He takes two steps forward. The driver jumps down and approaches the door. The flaps are drawn so no one can see inside. He opens the door and with a fancy sweep of his arm, invites the ladies to climb down. Then he retreats. The delvers now form a crowd around the wagon moving to get spots from where they can watch the ordeal. Suddenly all is silent.

Rosa climbs down first. She is dressed in a long blue dress with a hat skew on her lush blonde hair. She walks up to Cohen and they talk swiftly to each other. Then she turns back to the coach and gives a signal. One by one the girls emerge and are greeted with thunderous applause. First Michelle, pretty in pink. She naughtily pulls her dress up when she climbs down so that her legs show. The men scream and whistle. She smiles and blows kisses. She joins Rosa and Cohen. Then Anita, with a white dress that contrasts sharply with her dark complexion and black hair. She peeps around from under her dark lashes without smiling. Graciously she descents the steps, wave once, and under loud applause takes her place next to Michelle. Sophie smiles when she descents with her light green dress, hesitates for a moment on the last step, waves with both hands to the audience, takes her dress on both sides, lift it slightly, and with quick steps joins Rosa and the rest. The men enjoy themselves. They cheer and clap their hands. It is quite a show.

The Aletta comes down. It is such a beautiful picture that there is a moment of silence. In a yellow dress with frills that looks as if it was cast on her body and with the yellow ribbon in her long brown hair, her sun-tanned face, and perfect features, she is a picture. She is marvellous. A real beauty. This is the girl who I gladly will marry and brag with her by all, many of the young men think. Then they boldly begin to clap their hands.

Cohen is very excited. He turns to Rosa.

"The four girls are exceptional. You have done well, my dear."

"Wait! There is another one!"

"Another one?" She gestures that he must be quiet. The men start to talk among themselves and spin jokes.

Rosa holds up her hand. It is quiet. All are looking in expectation at the door of the coach. Then she is there. Flaming red in her red dress, red hair bound up with a ribbon. She stops on the first step, showing her voluptuous body. The men are gasping for breath. Rosa smiles. That is exactly what she wanted and Angelique doesn't disappoint her. She thoroughly enjoys these dramatic moments. Smiling and with swaying hips, she walks to the rest of the group, slowly so that the men can savour every step. She turns around and waves like a queen to her subjects. The crowd roars and jumps up and down and clap their hands. What a show!

Cohen is astounded. Where does this come from? At this moment he doesn't care. They are here! That's all that matters and he can raise his prices a bit. The diggers will come and feast their eyes on these beauties regularly.

"A free drink for all!" he shouts. "But the girls you won't see tonight. They must rest."

Chapter 14: The match

The hall of the hotel resembles a fairyland. Lanterns hang all over the place and yellow light shines through the room. On the tables against the walls are thick candles in tin holders. The tables are covered with tablecloths on which the diggers cheerfully spill beer and brandy. Cohen doesn't care about that. He rubs his small hands pleased with all the money he is going to make tonight. It was a good week on the diggings and those that haven't gone home for the weekend, and also the permanent delvers, the bankers, and others are all here. The excitement of the arrival of the cancan dancers is still in the air. It was one of the subjects that have continually been discussed; about which jokes were made and over which was argued who the queen of the beauties was.

It is the evening of the arm-wrestling match.

In the centre of the room are four tables with two chairs each on a side, and two candles on each table. Only the best are going to compete tonight. The heats have been dealt with in the canteens during the week and they all know who the strongest competitors are. Cohen delays the start of the match a bit. There are a few empty tables against the walls and the drinks are flowing. Another round or two will do just fine for his purse. Eventually, all the tables are full and he feels the unruly mood of the delvers. He walks to the stairs that wind upwards to the second floor and ascend some stairs. It is his podium.

"Guys," he yells but his voice is not loud enough. Someone at one table sees that his mouth opens and closes. He jumps on the table and whistles. The noise dies down.

"My good men," Cohen immediately takes his chance, "it is the big competition evening. Welcome to all of you and I hope we are going to have a good competition."

The men whistle, cheer, and clap their hands. Cohen holds his hands in the air. Silence follows. Shortly he explains the simple rules and gives the names of the judges at the tables. The four judges take their places at their respective tables. Only guys that have qualified are competitors tonight. Their names are printed on a list. Each one has only one chance. It works on a knock-out basis. After the first round, only the winners will compete further up to the end when only two will remain. The winner then is the great champion of the evening and he gets the prize money. If there is anyone at the end that reckons he can take on the champion, he can dare him.

"We will be starting in a few minutes. Make sure your glasses are full or that you have a bottle on the table. And may the best man win!"

A deafening cheer follows and the men call the waiters or go to the bar to fill up. Quite a nice party; the hard work and worries of the diggings forgotten.

One of the judges takes a list out of his pocket and walks to the farthest table. He hits with a spoon on a pan. The match is about to start.

"Table 1," he says loudly and points at the table next to him: "Izak Groenewald and Gary Hickley."

The men whistle as the competitors walk over the floor to the table.

The next table's names are announced and so the third and fourth. The competitors take their seats. On each table are two short candles burning. The flames flicker yellow and lusty as if they also join in the excitement. Between the tables of the spectators, the bookies move around and quickly writes down bets.

The men at the tables make ready. They massage their arm muscles and clamp their hands. Then the hands grip each other, elbows on the tables. Tension fills the place. It is dead still.

Suddenly the judge hits the pan loudly. At once tension sits in the arms and in the eyes of the spectators. Then it develops in power against power, bulging muscles, hands gripping firmly. Some try different techniques, sits askew on their chairs, others struggle and wrestle with grimaced faces and sweat on their foreheads. Others press air through their lips, their neck muscles bulging and groan like oxen that pull too heavy a load. The evening is young and if they want to stay in the competition, they now must quickly down the opponent.

"Damn!" one of the competitors shouts when the hairs on the back of his hand are scorched by the flame of the candle. He releases his grip and the tension in his arm becomes a lameness running down his arm. The winner's arm is held up by the judge. The spectators applaud. The evening promises to be quite something. One after the other the winners are announced.

The second group is announced. Kobus is at table 1. He holds his breath when his opponent's name is announced. It mustn't be Costa.

"Arend Liebenberg," the judge reads from the list. Kobus smiles. Costa is at table 2.

Arend is completely taken by surprise. As soon as the spoon hits the pan, and he tightens his grip around Kobus' hand, he feels how one mighty push moves his arm as if he has no control over it. He swears when Kobus holds his hand over the flame moments longer than necessary. Kobus laughs as Arend jumps up. He rubs his hand and then starts to laugh also. With his thumb, he shows that he has respect for the way Kobus has won. At least he now knows on who to bet his money. But Kobus' attention is elsewhere.

Costa has a young giant from the Cape as an opponent. Definitely a man who has scorched many hands. He is not allowing Costa to overrun him with brute force. That is why he tenses his strong muscles and let Costa do the pushing. I will let him struggle and tire his arm, he thinks. And in a while, I will push him down and burn his hand. But then he hears something like a soft blowing noise through Costa's lips. The next moment he feels something like an unstoppable wall pushing his arm as if he is pushed away from the table. Amazed he looks at the ugly, dark face of Costa, sees how a smile forms on his lips, feels as if his arm is not his anymore. When the burn is too intense, he relaxes and lets go. He looks at Costa admiringly. The man is a devil! He surely is going to win tonight.

The other tables also finish. When Costa passes Kobus, he shows him an obscene sign. The spectators see it and know what it means. Costa hopes Kobus goes through to the final round so that he can scorch him. Kobus only smiles and goes to his seat.

Round after round finishes. Then there are only eight competitors, then four and eventually, there are only two left. One of them is going to be the big champion. Costa or Kobus.

There is a ten-minute recess. The spectators fill up quickly and the bookies are busy. It is not easy to say who the winner will be. Neither of them had noteworthy opposition. They are not too tired and both look fit and able. It promises to be a mammoth contest.

When the spoon hits the pan, the noise of the spectators reduces to a sociable buzz. Now and then some of them burst out laughing for a witticism from one of the spectators.

"Now you will see the Porra poop!"

"Kobus will piss like one of his oxen, I tell you!"

"How does a Portuguese smell when he burns?"

"I hear Kobus brought his coffin from the bay."

As soon as the hands grip, it becomes dead quiet. With in-held breaths, they watch hoping this match will not end in an anti-climax. They are not disappointed. The arms stay upright. The movements from one side to the other are minimal. Power cancels power. They stay in deadly balance. The faces are grim and tensed. The eyes fixed rigidly in one place as to not lose concentration. It is clear: either enormous technique or perseverance is going to clinch this match.

Suddenly the wet hand of the two contestants slip out of each other's grip and waves over the table. They rise and towels are handed to them. They dry their hands, their arms, and their faces. Again they dry their hands thoroughly.

"Okay, guys," the judge says. Their hands clamp. He hits the pan. They test each other's power, strain of the highest order. For quite a few minutes it is muscle against muscle, will against will, strength against strength. No one budges. The spectators are spell-bound.

Then Kobus's face shows pain as if he gets a cramp in one of his arm's muscles. A small smile plucks at Costa's mouth corners. Then he delves deep and gathers another bit of strength. Slowly, but slowly, he pushes Kobus' hand over. His face lights up, he smiles the smile of the victor. Kobus holds up his hand. He has lost.

The cheers are long and loud. Especially from those who have placed their bets correctly. Cohen comes and holds Costa's arm in the air. Then he leads him to a table where he can rest.

"You can pay out," someone yells at Cohen, "no one can match this ugly Portuguese!"

"There won't be another challenger," another says and rub his arm as if he has been in the contest himself. With the tension broken, the guys start to talk exuberantly and make sure that their glasses are filled. The contest is being analyzed in fine detail and there are speculations about the cramp that Kobus seemingly encountered.

"No," one of hem concludes after a big swig of his brandy, "the Porra is just too strong, that's' all."

Fifteen minutes of noise passes. Cohen walks over to Costa who drinks one glass of water after the other. They talk and Costa nods. He is ready for a challenger if there is one. He greedily looks at the prize money which

Cohen has in a pouch in his hand. Cohen winks at the judge. Kobus turns slightly in his chair and winks at Chris.

The judge hit his pan. Silence follows. Cohen speaks.

"As you all know, our rules are that our champion can be challenged. If there is no one, he is the victor of the evening and all the prize money goes to him." He taps on the pouch he holds in front of him. The men applaud.

Cohen smiles satisfied. The evening is a great success. The prize money will easily be covered by his betting on Costa. He gestures to the judge. He hits his pan.

"If there is no one to challenge Mr. Costa …"

"Here is one!" Chris's voice from the corner carries through the hall. He stands up. Some nearly drop from their chairs to turn around and try to see who it is.

"There is someone?" Cohen is baffled.

"Yes, my brother Samuel."

"Samuel?"

Chris drags Samuel up. "Here he is. He challenges Costa."

Samuel slowly and reluctantly rises. Cohen can see it is a big man, but he wonders. A real farm boy.

"Gentlemen, we have a challenger. His name is Samuel …"

"Strydom!" Chris calls over the floor and pushes him ahead.

"Okay, then. It will be Samuel Strydom against Mister Costa. Let's give them some time to get ready." What he really means is, get your drinks and do your betting.

While Chris pushes the unwilling Samuel over the floor, the men value his chances. A farm boy, unknown, maybe a fortune hunter. He seems to be big and strong but he will short technique, and experience surely, but maybe … most of them quickly place their bets on Costa. Kobus calls one of the bookies and whispers in his ear. The man is amazed but says nothing and only writes in his booklet. He then proceeds to the next client.

Suddenly the sound of the pan. Costa has already reached the table. The candles are lit. Tension fills the hall. The men take great swigs. There is always some excitement in the unknown.

Costa has a big grimace on his face that says: you ignorant, little shit, how dare you take on someone like me? Samuel has no expression on his face. He has been pushed in at the deep side. It was so sudden, he doesn't realize fully what has happened. Sometimes his brain works very slowly. All that he knows is that if he wins, Kobus, according to Chris, promised to give him fifty pounds. And then the prize money would also be his. He opens and closes his big right hand, rub his arm muscles with his left hand, and takes his seat. All that he remembers is Chris' last words: don't let him trick you. Hold him and push slowly. You can do it!

When Costa's hand grips his, he feels the tremendous strength in it. His courage ebbs. He looks around and catches Kobus's eyes. Kobus thumb up for him and nods. That helps. Samuel shifts and gets his sitting right.

The spoon suddenly clangs against the pan. Instantly he feels how immense strength pushes his arms sideways. He is amazed to see their hands move. Costa's hand is an iron clamp. Only with immense will-power, he can curtail the movement but he feels lameness in his shoulder. Intuitively he tries to stop the movement but it is still going, albeit very slowly. He can't push now, he must just defend. His eyes are fixated on Costa's ugly face, the big nose, the unshaven beard, the thin grinning, challenging lips. And then he sees the mockery in Costa's eyes.

Instantly Costa becomes his step-dad that wants to force him to lower his arm; to capitulate; to burn him on the candle; who laughs at him because he has no choice than to be obedient. Resentment and rebellion well up in him and together with it his fighting spirit. It runs through his painful shoulder, through the muscles of his upper arm down to the strained muscles of his forearm down to his hand. He now is looking Costa fiercely in the eyes. He tightens his grip on Costa's hand and his muscles contracts. Fraction for fraction he moves Costa's arm back to vertical where they keep each other for quite a while. Costa's face changes. The grin leaves his mouth, his dark eyes widen in amazement. Then he sees how the young man grits his teeth, and how his arm moves almost invisible to the eye. He feels how his wrist is bending and he knows, he has lost already. Here is more strength than he can muster but that easily he doesn't give up. One or two times he tries to delve for more strength, but it only helps to retard the movement a little. Then the boy starts to push relentlessly down.

Costa is also a real sportsman. Suddenly he acknowledges defeat by pulling his hand out of Samuel's grip.

So sudden was the defeat that Samuel is surprised. Costa stands up, walks around the table, take his arm, and let him stand up. Then he holds Samuel's arm in the air. He has respect for more power than his.

"Whoa, Uncle, you are strong," Samuel says simply.

Costa bursts out in laughter and taps him on the shoulder. "And you is more strong," he says in crooked English.

Chapter 15: Caprini in New Rush

Caprini is in a foul mood when he arrives in New Rush. He has pains all over his body. He had to travel on the wooden chest of a wagon from Algoa Bay sitting on that hard and splintered wood. There was no place for him on the wagon. That was laden to the brink with building material for corrugated iron houses in New Rush. And he thinks that backward Boer asked him way too much for the uncomfortable ride. Many times he had to climb down and walked alongside when the oxen trekked to heavily uphill or when the wheels of the heavy ox-wagon threatened to sink away in loose sand.

And the sun! Good heavens, it burns down mercilessly. The wide rim hat only helped to keep the sun away from his face, but when the sun like hellfire stands still at noon, then your clothes become wet rags that cling to your sweaty body. Under your hat, it feels as if your brains are cooking. At night it becomes so cold that you lie and shiver with only a thin blanket over you.

And the ugly scenery. Where is Canada with its breathtaking mountains, crystals hanging from the trees, the lush green valleys in the summer, and crystal clear streams falling down the mountains? Here are only bare plains, with ill-formed thorn trees and sparse grass. Waterholes and fountains are far apart. How these people know where to go to get to the right place, is a miracle. For him, all these places look the same.

And the dust! When the west wind blows in the afternoon, it looks as if handsful of dust raise into the air so that you must cover your face with a cloth to prevent suffocation. Can there be any gems in this part of the world? No, really, what has come over him that he wanted to come to this dry country? Maybe the diamond story is an old wife's tale. Maybe another Eldorado illusion.

However, they will not order houses if there is nothing. With that, he had to console himself when his chafed buttocks glowed, when he spat the sand from his mouth, when he felt like an ox hide parched by the sun.

When they arrived, he was surprised. It is quite a town. The houses, the few shops, and canteens are more or less orderly placed; not so haphazard as he had experienced in Canada's delver's camps. The basic infrastructure was there, the place has at least one bank and a post office, the police have a new office and there are hotels and lodges. The town is bustling. Ox wagons move in relentlessly with high laden loads.

The wheels are turning. He sees the claims on one side and heaps of gravel that have been sifted. Yes, the wheels are turning. There is hope.

First, he has to find out how things work here. Who are the men pulling the strings? Who are the ones making money? He knows diggings by now. Mostly only a few diggers become wealthy and even more wealthy as time goes by. Sometimes it is a man who obtains his wealth by cheating the stupid, the strugglers. Even if you give those idiots rich claims with diamonds or gold, they will still make a mess of it. Those are the guys you must exploit and relieve them from their riches. They can't handle it anyway.

Caprini visits all the boarding houses. He compares prices. He doesn't care about neatness and cleanliness. As soon as he is making money, he can move to a better lodging. After he has stashed his belongings, he walks by all the canteens. It is in these places where you get the most valuable information. When alcohol unties men's lips, they talk. You can get a heap of information. Then you must separate facts from shit.

Many of the people speak in a language he doesn't understand, but he listens carefully. He hears the names Rhodes and Rudd. He shifts onto a stool in a bar next to one of the blabbermouths.

"This man, Rhodes, who is he?" he asks in his best English and winks at the barman to pour a drink for the guy.

The red-faced man turns to him and looks him straight in the face.

"Who wants to know?" he askes bluntly. This must be a foreigner, a Greek, Portuguese, or what have you.

"I am Caprini. I am an Italian." Whether it was a good idea to introduce himself he doesn't know.

The man looks at him attentively but holds out his glass for the barman to fill. He will only divulge information in bits. Maybe he can earn a few more drinks. His English in any case is not so fluent.

"Rhodes is an Englishman. Many stories about him are doing the round. He comes from Natal."

"Natal?"

"Yes, in the east on the coast on the other side of the Drakens Mountains" Caprini nods. He doesn't make out head or tail. But it is not important.

"The guys say he wanted to do some business over there but it was a failure …" he continues. "They say …"

Caprini listens patiently. Okay, if Rhodes is the big guy here, it is worth a few drinks.

After a lot of useless information, Caprini asks: "But why is he such an important man here?"

"His brother has a claim here and he and his partner Rudd seems to me have the most brains here. They buy and sell diamonds. He and his brother have already founded a company. It is the biggest here. There are also some smaller companies because the individual claims are becoming too deep to work alone. He tells everyone that he plans to get hold of the greatest part of the mine. Only a few people know it but he is already talking of buying out claims on a great scale. His machinery to work the claims deeper down is on its way from England."

The man is still going on about the mining, the heaps of ground that have to be moved, and what have you. Caprini has heard enough. Rhodes is the man to watch. He will probably have a circle of friends or colleagues gathered around him. He will have to try to break into this group.

He pays for the drinks and walks out in the cool night air. From somewhere comes music, loud applause, and shouting. He walks to the hotel. The hotel has a big lounge with small tables for its clientele. The place is full of delvers. At the opposite end from where he entered a stage has been erected now closed behind curtains. The music has stopped.

He walks in and sits down at a small table on the left. He would have liked to get some supper but it seems only drinking is the order of the day or evening. At a big table next to his at the wall, seven or eight young men are heartily celebrating. Frequently one of them proposes a toast and then they drink lustily from their glasses. Then one calls a waiter for another bottle.

He doesn't understand what they are on but it is clear that they are very excited about something. Then he sees it. The one who has ordered the bottle takes out his handkerchief, hold it in the palm of his hand, and unfolds it slowly. Caprini cannot clearly see but guesses it is a diamond. From the shouting, he can make out that it is something exceptional. Then the young man takes the diamond between his thumb and forefinger and sways his hand in front of the others to see. They cheer him loudly. Then he puts it back in his hand and folds it in his handkerchief.

They all laugh and scream and drink their glasses empty in one swig.

You stupid little shit, Caprini thinks, show them what you have and tonight when you are as drunk as a skunk and walks out of here, someone hits you over the head with a spade and take your diamond. He shakes his head.

The next moment the music starts. It is a player on an old honky-tonk piano to the left side of the stage. The diggers clap their hands. The curtains open. The stage is bare. Then out come three girls and with quick steps jogs over the stage and start with their moves. The men whistle and applaud.

In time with the music, they step left and then right, kick high up so that their colourful petticoats waves through the air, and their legs are shown.

The crowd roars their enjoyment. Caprini watches for a while but then fatigue overtakes him. He walks out, goes to his room, and hits the sack.

Chapter 16: Philip Shaw senior

My Dearest Philip

I hope this letter reaches you in good health. I arranged for money to be transferred to you the last time I was in Colesburg. Since my last letter to you very bad things happened to me.

But first of all, I wrote to the judge president in the Cape, an old friend of mine, and ask him to give you a good appointment as soon as you are back. I gave him your address. I hope he will write to you. That is to say, if you want to come back and not stay in England. I won't blame you as you so wish. As it appears to me, my life is about to end soon.

The Strydom boys left me in the lurch terribly. One Sunday afternoon while taking a nap, they stole money and vanished completely. I don't know where they have gone and Ragie can't tell me also. You know her, the Griqua woman that works in the house. After everything I have done for them, they dropped me so horribly and also took my money. The police on Colesburg, being part of the Cape, says they have no jurisdiction to investigate cases in the Free State Republic and I believe they wouldn't have gone to English territory. Maybe they are now north over the Vaal River in the South African Republic.

I struggled on. Luckily the housekeeper's brother helped with milking, but I have to tend the animals. Then a horrible thing happened. I had a sort of a stroke, was in hospital for a time in Colesburg. Now I am on the farm again but my left arm is lame, I can only move him slightly. My leg was also bad but is better now. I can walk with a crutch. My mouth is skew, I can' look for myself in a mirror.

I had to allow the housekeeper's family to come and stay on the farm but they are a lazy lot. Sheep disappear and some have been caught by leopards. A few of my best heifers also disappeared. I think they stole it. Of the crops on the land comes nothing. It is now overgrown by weed. The maize we probably can cut for feed but I see trouble for the winter ahead. Maybe I must sell the farm and move to Colesburg. There I can be cared for if things become too bad.

Don't for my sake interrupt your training and if you want to study further, as you mentioned in your last letter, do it. There is enough money to see you through. But you must decide for yourself. Think about your future. At this stage, you will know what is best for you.

Your loving father.

Philip.

Amazed Philip stared at the letter from the Cape. Official, with a stamp of His Majesty on the envelope. From the office of the Judge President.

He was even more flabbergasted about the contents. The President wrote that his old friend, Philip's dad, had written to him and told him that his son's studies are nearing their end. He is very glad about that. It is good for a young man in law to be well trained in English law. Especially in the Cape Colony where they sometimes struggle to find good lawyers. I any case, there are different posts vacant but the most crucial is that they need a prosecutor for the Circuit Court in the Northern Cape and when the magistrate is appointed at New Rush, he must be stationed there. The Northern Cape is a vast area and difficult to control and it is necessary to establish law and order there. New Rush is becoming a rather big place with all sorts of characters because of the diamonds and frequently there are reports of all sorts of criminalities that won't be curtailed without thorough law enforcement.

If he was interested, he should write so that his appointment could be arranged.

Philip lovingly thought of his father and longed for him. His dad did so much for him. The best schools in the Cape. Supplying money for him to study in England. He lost his mother early in his life, but his father tried to compensate for his loss by giving him only the best. He longed for the farm. Although he was only there on holidays, it was a great pleasure. Always there was a new horse or livestock specially earmarked for him.

He had no affinity for the woman his father married again. She was a meek woman, staying in the background, but she looked well after his father. For him, she was merely a white housekeeper in the house. He never thought of her as a wife for his father. Her three sons and he didn't meet eye to eye. There was the language difference and also the cultural difference. He was raised in the proud British tradition, they were simple farm boys. According to him, they could not even converse properly and he despised their common way of making jokes about him. They ignored him most of the time but he could feel that they are making jokes behind his back.

However, it bothered him not too much. He treated them like servants and thereby showed his superiority. As far as he was concerned, they were dependent on the benevolence of his father, especially after their mother had died.

And now he is sitting and reading his father's letter.

He is sitting in a warm pub, drinking one whiskey after the other. The noise of the clients around the other tables and their joking and laughing for him is non-existent. His whole mood is filled to the brim with hatred.

The despicable dogs. It is as his father said, after everything he had done for them, they dropped him badly. And then even to take his money! Thieves, miscreants, cockroaches! The offspring of a bad Dutch generation! His hands open and close. If he just could lay his hands on them, the lowly hoodlums!

He realizes now that his father's letter, and also the one from the Cape, has changed his life irrevocably. He must go back to South Africa as soon as possible. He must get to his dad, he must decide what has to be done with his father and with the farm.

He reads the letter again. It is true, he has considered staying in England longer and while he completes his service year at an excellent law practice, study further. However, he must admit, he longs for his dad, to the tranquillity of the farm, to his horse which he can race through the fields, to the buggy with the two horses in front that leisurely jogs while the iron knaves crush over the ground. He must admit; he is tired of the English weather, the long and bitter winters, the mist that enfolds you, and the buildings that seem to smother you. Not so long ago he slipped on the sleet and nearly broke his leg. He had to struggle for weeks with a sore ankle. And he is tired of the food. Soup, broth, cabbage, and only little pieces of meat. In his mind, he could see the brown roasted leg of lamb, with roasted potatoes and rice, strings of sausages, and biltong. Fresh vegetables from the garden and cold ginger ale on a scorching day.

Yes, he takes a last swig from the glass, he must get to his father as soon as possible.

Chapter 17: Arrangements, smuggling and entertainment

Costa is sitting at the table occupying almost half of his side. His big, round face smiles, his mighty forearms rest on the table, and in his fist, he clamps a glass of brandy.

"Wrestling, you must learn wrestling."

"Wrestle?"

"Wrestle, big sport, big money. All over the land."

"What about boxing?" Chris wants to know.

"Boxing, Chris, no good," says Costa. He pulls away his lip with his finger and shows them a broken tooth. He again closely looks at Samuel. No, boxers learn to fight from a young age; you must be able to hit fast and dug quickly. Samuel doesn't seem to be able to do it even if he can break a man's jaw in two places with one hit of his mighty fist. No, boxing needs years of experience. With wrestling it is different. Your strength is your main feature. Technique also counts but that can be learned more easily. Strength is the basis and Samuel has that in abundance. Techniques he will coach him.

Costa explains as best he can in broken English how he envisages the thing. He has been wrestling for years but his age is counting. All over the country wrestling competitions are held and the winner pockets handsomely but the big money is in gambling, more so when you have an unknown competitor.

"But he must help here on the diggings." Chris is not at all satisfied. Samuel is a big part of the plan he is constructing from they have arrived. Herklaas is lost to the plan by working at the printer and he will never convince him to be part of his plan. Samuel must be working on the claims. That will give him enough of an excuse to move between the claims. Between the claims and the banks, diamonds move with people. And these people can be departed of their gems quite easily. There should be clever ways to achieve this. He is in no way going to toil and sweat as he did on Shaw's farm for nothing. He made quite a lot from the arm-wrestling match. It must be the start of a profitable business. He must just use his cunning.

"OK," Costa reluctantly capitulates. "In day he works the claim. After work, I teach him to wrestle, Okay?"

For now, Chris is satisfied.

Early in the morning, they team to the claims. They crawl out of their houses, huts, shacks, and shelters. Each morning the glitter of diamonds shines in their eyes. Yesterday a few guys unearthed a few beauties. Those with money invest in better equipment and gathers more diamonds than those with their primitive utensils that let beauties slip past. Every day they dig and excavate and wash with the hope that the big one will lie there like a glittering star in the sieve amongst the grey stones. Big, strong men are in demand. The sooner the gravel can be processed, the better and the bigger the chance of success.

Chris has done his homework thoroughly during the past month. One of the most successful diggers is the German, rather Austrian, Baron Von Holstein. He is a middle-aged man and is only halfway engaged with his claims. He is stinking rich. He and his brother inherited a salt mine, but after he and his conservative brother quarreled because of his brother's contempt of the baron's licentious lifestyle, they arranged for his half to be taken over by his brother. He pocketed an enormous lot of money for that and every month a handsome payment lands in his bank account.

He is a big man, with a rough, red beard, a big mouth, and a mighty voice you can hear from miles around. Everyone is a little afraid of him, especially of that blue eyes that seem to look directly into your soul. That is why his claims are successful. When he goes down to his claims late in the afternoon, few men dare to be dishonest. If he is satisfied with the day's work, he happily goes to Cohen's hotel and consumes gallons of beer and whisky.

This evening he is sitting at a table near the stage. Cohen announced earlier that tonight would be extra special. After a month the dancers have been trained properly, they all have new clothes and they are going to entertain the men on the latest dances from Europe. He is very much looking forward to it and he likes to order more than enough liquor and treat his mates.

He is even more content tonight. Not only did he hire Samuel to look after the workers, but he also did well today. The shining gems are in his inner pocket in a leather pouch and he must contain himself not to open the pouch and look at the marvellous diamonds. Life is good for him. The diamond diggings are good to him. In his crooked Dutch he spins one joke or anecdote after the other from his colorful history in between his phenomenal onslaught on the alcoholic beverages.

"Drink, man, drink!" he shouts when he sees how Samuel reluctantly sips his whisky. This giant brings him luck, he thinks. With him at his claims, nothing will go wrong. The whole New Rush knows it is Samuel who humiliated Costa. And that is no mean feat. With his strength to break a men's neck as easily as a match stick, no one would dare to try and trick him.

Chris is nursing his drink. He has only half an ear for the big man's babbling. He is very satisfied. His negotiations with the big man went well. Samuel is now a sort of foreman on the claims of the baron.

"You must make sure you have a good foreman to watch the workers. Or else the bright stones jump into another man's pocket. The guys are afraid of Samuel. They won't take chances with him. I will also keep an eye to make sure everything goes well."

The baron indeed was happy to shift responsibilities to others. He and Chris made a sort of partnership. They will look after the claims. If the baron allows it he can be helpful with the selling of the diamonds, Chris suggested, but the baron put his foot down. No, it was so satisfying to walk with a pouch of diamonds in his pocket. It gives him something to shout about and impress all. And to walk into the bank and looking important while selling his diamonds, is like a balm for his massive ego.

He is also a formidable hunter. The arrangement with Chris gives him even more time to engage in his favourite pastime.

Chris also is quite content for another reason. It was really good luck that he met Staanvas. He went to buy something in one of the grocery shops to eat. When he came out, he saw the slim man immediately. The way he peeped from under his ragged hat, told Chris that this man would never take up a shovel.

Curiously he walked nearer.

"Don't you dig in the claims?" It was a way to initiate a conversation.

The black eyes only peeked at him. He is being weighed, Chris knew. Maybe the man wouldn't even talk to him.

"No, I don't dig. They hit me and broke my ribs."

Chris could see he was holding one arm as if it was in a sling.

"Now you are just standing around?" Chris continued. He instinctively knew this is a man you should get acquainted with. He didn't look like one of the brown or black workers. He appeared to be far more intelligent. His skin was lighter and he had a sharp, almost aristocratic nose. Somewhere and maybe not so long ago, there was European blood, Chris surmised.

"Now I stand just here for a small happening." The words are chosen carefully, but he could see his words tickled a flicker of attention. Therefore, he continues. "Dutchman, you don't perhaps have a small thing to smoke?" he steered the conversation in another direction. If there was no reaction, then he would know there was nothing. If the man didn't want to talk to him again, he would simply walk off. Chris took out his leather tobacco pouch and pour some tobacco in his hand palm.

"Here," he says. "Do you have something for me?"

Staanvas didn't answer straightforward. He held out his hand and Chris scratched the tobacco onto his palm. Then he took a little bone pipe out of his pocket. Only when the smoke fumes hung in the late afternoon air, he answered carefully.

"Maybe I have, maybe not."

"Let's walk so that we can talk."

Staanvas indeed had something. Whether he had stolen it, bribed someone to get hold of it, or gambled it out of someone, wasn't Chris' concern. When they were at a place no one could see them, Staanvas took out a pouch and handed it over.

Five smallish diamonds in the pouch. Beautiful!

"Where did you get it?" Chris asked amazed, but he knew he wouldn't get an answer. It was a stupid question. "Must I sell it for you?"

No answer. It means yes.

"Good. Where do I find you?"

"You don't find me; I find you. And don't try to cheat me. I know what they are worth." The black eyes roamed the grass plains as if he doesn't care but from his soft voice, Chris deducts that he is quite sincere. He shivers. He has heard enough stories of how a knife can be buried between one's ribs.

"You can trust me. We must do business again."

Chris now touches the diamonds in the pouch in his pocket. He knows what to do.

The piano man starts. The first two dancers appear. Samuel freezes in his chair. Aletta! He has so many times just sit and watched her, seen her in the streets, and admired her. The other night at the wrestling match he won easily, to the great joy of Costa, he was aware of her eyes on him and that gave him extra motivation to clinch the match. He knows what he can do with his powerful body and how he can throw his opponents around like wet bags. He also knows how he can work workers under the dust with a shovel, he knows his body is young strong and manly, but if she looks at him with the slight heartache in her green eyes, then his legs become limp sprouts that threaten to fold right under him. He doesn't know how to handle the fierce emotions filling his inside. In his more than twenty-two years he has never experienced this.

Aletta and Michelle are doing the first show. It is a tune with a quick rhythm and quick steps that they mirror-like neatly and nimbly execute. From behind the curtain, Rosa peeps satisfied. These two are jewels. They match each other and it is as if they from the start found each other's rhythm and support each other. Of all the girls it is only Angelique who wants to dance solo so that she gets all the attention. Not that Rosa mind at all, she is voluptuous and the men are mad about her. She allows her this somewhat to do her own thing except in the group items. There she demands absolute discipline. It is not cheap bordello shows. It is a proper hotel and a proper cabaret. It can't be ordinary. They have to compete with Dutoitspan. There Stafford-Parker built a handsome building in which shows take place. There is also a new hotel with billiard rooms and a giant lounge where concerts are held. The people of Dutoitspan look down on New Rush and its buildings which look sloppy with unorderly living areas and many bordellos and canteens.

Aletta sees the young man at the table and looks directly at him while she and Michelle execute their lightning-fast steps. She has seen him and admired him. Such a strong body. With him, she will feel safe. He will be able to protect her. For her, he is a wonder man.

The two finished their show. Costa comes and sits with them. Immediately the baron starts a joke. "A Frenchman," he says, "washes his hands and then he pees. An Englishman pees and then washes his hands. A Portuguese washes his hands while he pees."

His laugh bellows through the hall. The others laugh with him. Costa also laughs heartily. He could not make out one word of the baron's Dutch-German, but it must be funny. That's why he also laughs. The baron pours him a heavy whisky and hits him against his upper arm.

"Do you want to hear another joke about the Portuguese?"

Wildeboer cuts in: "Look over there."

The baron turns his head and looks. Four men sit around a table talking earnestly. One of them is quite excited and points with his forefinger to the rest.

"Who are they?" Chris asks.

"The smallish man pointing with his forefinger is Aylward. A stubborn Irishman. Tells people that he killed a policeman in Manchester. Maybe it is just bragging, but when he came here at first he pretended to be a doctor but he is no doctor's ass. No medical qualifications. Has been in jail here for manslaughter. Real pest, I tell you!" The baron takes a deep breath and a big swig of beer.

"The others, let me see. Von Schlickman, Ling and Henry Tucker seems to me ..." he continues.

"Now what about them?" asks Chris out of turn. The baron looks at him fiercely. He doesn't like to be interrupted.

"I smell problems. Keep your eyes open and your ears to the ground. The Irishman has it mainly against the black diggers. He is also against the taxes from the government and also against the blacks that work the gravel heaps to find diamonds. I hear he is already busy to weaponize some of his followers."

"But what is his real problem?" Samuel wants to know.

"As I understand it," Wildeboer cuts in, "he is against the allocation of claims to coloureds but mainly against the commissionaires that Barkley employed here. He, and many others, feel that the old delver's associations did good work because they knew the delver's problems. They believe Barkly wants to undermine the authority of the delvers. Further, he stokes revolution. I think ..."

The loud notes of the piano and then the shrill sound of a violin that cuts through the hall, makes Wildeboer's words inaudible.

Herklaas is coming into the hall, searching for the group where his brothers are. Shyly he walks through the hall and is amazed to see the exuberance of even the timidest digger. The evening is loaded with expectation. He sees them sitting near the stage and has to force himself not to turn and run away. It is strange and it is a special evening and he is still afraid of strange things.

His boss literally had to chase him away from the office.

"Are you finished?" He was.

"Then go to the hotel. I'm going now. I hear it is a special evening."

"I'll rather …"

Then Wildeboer got annoyed. His temper can flare up sometimes instantly.

"You can't sit here like a fucking silly ape. My hell, boy! What a jerk you are! You don't look to me like one of those other boys. Go and enjoy yourself! Aah," he grinned complacently. "My young days with the beautiful Dutch maidens! Get the hell out of here before I bang your head against the door!"

He turned and left. Herklaas has learned that Jans Wildeboer's bark is far worse than his bite. He has a way to say the most insulting things without really meaning it. He is really good for him. Give him food and a roof over his head and a weekly salary. What he doesn't know is that Jans say a thank you prayer for this quite, hardworking boy. Without him, he would surely have seen his ass.

Herklaas slowly walks through the hall and is amazed at the spectators. They are fixated on a group of dancers with colourful frill dresses kicking high in the air and rhythmically moving from side to side over the stage, then form arty patterns and eventually in pairs bow to the audience with Angelique in the centre shaking her frill dress and then throwing her arms in the air when the music comes to an end.

Thunderous applause follows. The men whistle and clap their hands. Herklaas quickly moves to the table. Chris offers him a chair. As soon as he sits down the baron puts a glass of whisky in his hand.

"You are working for the Dutchman!" the baron shouts. Herklaas nods. It wasn't a question really.

The baron roars further: "Funny crowd here. Dutchmen, English, Portuguese, and a silly lot that call themselves Afrikaners. Even an Italian. What a mixture." He laughs heartily: "Caprini!" he yells to the table next to them, "how many Italians are here, or are you the only spaghetti guzzler?"

Caprini hears his name but he can't hear because of the noise around him and he doesn't understand the language the baron is using. Courteously his nods his head in the direction of the baron. Here are people you don't mess with. The baron is one of them. He is intelligent and big. There are other big guys as well like Costa and his learner. He doesn't care about them, by the way, he thinks they are low-class people.

Then his eyes catch Chris's. Chris gestures something. Just a small wave of his hand. He immediately recognizes it. Maybe Chris has something for him. He has seen Chris operating and trying to do business. For eye blind, Caprini bought a claim and got workers, but he is not planning to make money out of it. They say his claim is too far away from the main deposit. He stands by when they wash his gravel just to make sure he is not cheated but for the rest, he is not very interested in the claim. He works in the black market.

There are always illegal gems around and the guys that don't have claims must get rid of them. That is where he makes his money. He soon learned the value of the stones, their different qualities, and which generate the highest income. He knows that when a big stone is discovered it is on everyone's lips so it's not worth thinking about them. The smaller ones, but as pure as possible, are his forte. He buys them for half of its worth and sells it systematically to the bank. For unpure stones he pays next to nothing and percentage-wise makes more money out of it. His claim now and then brings in a few diamonds.

Suddenly the music starts again and Caprini's attention is caught by the dancers coming on to the stage. This time it is three of them, colourfully dressed with small umbrellos. It mesmerizes him. It's like Europe. Whoever could think that you would see such beauty in the wild west of Africa? And Aletta! Mama mia! What a gorgeous madonna! He thinks back to all the girls he had known, but no one enchanted him like this brunette. He compares her with the other two, Angelique and Anita. They are also beautiful and their movements are fluid, but they miss the grace of Aletta. For him, she is the princess, but also the shy fawn, the woman for whom you will fight your brother in a sword fight. He desires her with his whole being. He must have her for himself, come what may!

The show ends. He is still in ecstasy when he sees Chris moves past in front of him. He waits a while. Then he rises slowly, gestures to the others around the table he wants to go and pee outside. Behind the hotel in an open spot in the dim moonlight, Chris is waiting for him. Caprini stops next to him. In the manner in which he comes and stands next to him, Chris knows little conversation is necessary. He hands over the pouch to him.

Caprini feels in the pouch. "How much?" whispers Caprini.

Chris tells him.

"I shall have a look at them." He puts the pouch in his pocket and unbuttons his fly. Chris turns around and walks back to the hotel. He is just in time to see the final show with all five girls on the stage.

The tune is quick. The five girls come with quick steps on the stage with their frill dresses. Each one with a different colour in a row with their arms stretched out in front of them so that their finger points almost touch the one in front of her. They make snakes all over the stage while they now and then on a hard note of the music kick up at the back. Angelique with a bloodred dress is in front. The others follow with Aletta at the end.

Then they form a straight row with their fingertips touching, arms stretched out. Suddenly they bend forward and kick backward so that the frills of their dresses look like small, colourful waterfalls in the light. Then they stand up and kick high forward. First to the left and then to the right. Then they make a few quick steps left and right. They repeat the whole process. It is cancan at its best.

The men are enjoying the show immensely. This is really special. And this is the grand finale. They leave their tables and form a crowd in front of the stage while applauding loudly. The music becomes faster and the steps and high kicks are executed lightning fast. It is cancan at its best. The dresses are now being lifted high so that the legs are bare up to their knees. They wave the clutched material through the air from side to side.

They stop their kicking and go around in a circle. Angelique in front pretends to be falling off the stage. They go around in the circle again. The baron is the first to realize their intention and he steps forward.

Sideways Annelique drops in his arms. The other girls again go round in a circle and the next one falls into the arms of a waiting man. They repeat the process until only Aletta remains who is finally completing her circle.

When Angelique fell into the baron's arms, Caprini by wrestling through the men positioned himself to catch Aletta in his arms. He made sure that he stands against the stage with no one in front of him. Most of the guys are so intoxicated that it was an easy feat for him. Caprini watches her with greedy eyes as she takes the last circle and quick steps to the front of the stage. Within seconds, he knows, this angel will lie in his arms. He stretches out his arms in anticipation. She is at the front. Now!

A mighty hand grabs him by the shoulder and toss him aside like a rag doll. Samuel stands in his place. As Caprini lands on his back on the floor, he only sees how his angel falls into Samuel's strong arms.

For a moment Samuel is mildly surprised by the fact that he has moved so quickly and acted instantly. He only feels the soft body of this beauty against him, her arms around his neck, and her soft cheek against his. He is overwhelmed and stands dead still with her in his arms. The other girls have been carried off to the men's tables where they chat and guy with them. He wonders whether he should do the same.

"Let's go," she whispers in his ear. "Go over the stage. There is a side door to the street."

Her soft voice shakes him out of passivity. He carries her in his arms over the stage. The men shout and clap their hands. What a wonderful evening!

Moments later he puts her down outside the hotel. They walk down the street to a building further on. When the girls arrived, Cohen had to make provision for lodging for Aletta. He remembered a building down the street at the side of the hotel with an attic with steep wooden steps going up. It was a sort of storage space and the owner rented it to Cohen to accommodate Aletta. It was furnished for her. Only a bed and the most needed things, although quite cramped but it was heaven for her. It was privacy. After living in an ox-wagon, it was heaven on earth. She can lock the door and wash and no one would bother her.

At the foot of the steps he stops. He doesn't know what to do. It is so weird, so unreal, so exciting but how he must handle the situation isn't clear.

She takes his hand. "Come!" She leads him up the stairs, opens the door, pulls him inside, and closes the door. It is dark. Only the dim light of a quarter moon that stands on its tail cheekily comes through the small window. She can feel the uncertainty in his hand as if he wants to let go of it. She tightens her grip, leads him to her bed, and let him sit down.

She sits down next to him and starts to tell her story. Her history is unfolding before him. Her, mother, her father, their struggle in poverty for years, her father's death, Staanvas's help, and eventually Rosa and the dancers in New Rush. He puts his arms around her and hugs her tightly. I will defend you with my life!

"And Lion Head? What a funny name for a dog."

"At one stage, we were at the outspan of a trek herder. His Boerboel bitch had three pups. He wanted to keep two and kill the third one. 'Look at the miserable pup', he said, 'he has a head like a lion but a body like a meerkat with scabies.' 'I want him,' I said, that little lion head puppy. We called him Lion Head."

They laugh. Everything seems so natural. Then he starts his story.

Caprini is having a horrible night. Damn, backward farmer boy! Just because he has the power in his simple body, he thinks he can get what he wants. What an embarrassment! So much as the crowd has cheered Samuel, so much they have laughed at him. It is unforgivable! Deep in his heart, he swears revenge. He will think of a way, but for now, he sees in his mind's eye a dark deep dungeon beneath a castle with pain benches form the middle ages that can pull even the strongest man's limbs apart.

The worst is that he has lost her. He could already feel the soft, warm body against him, the hair caressing his cheek, his arms around her soft body. Then he flew through the air and landed unsophisticated a few yards further on the floor, while the bearded faces grimaced at him. He becomes aware that he holds a dagger in his right hand. He took it from a robber in a street fight in Rome, and cut him up with it. It is a dagger with a sharp, long blade that could slice in between the ribs into the heart of the enemy. It has a sharp blade that can diminish the life light out of the enemy's eyes in seconds. He stabs at the imaginary giant, sees how the blood stains the clothes, sees the pain on the distorted face, how the eyes afraid and in agony dim and eventually froze.

He feels better, his humiliation and anger in the meantime subsiding. He will make a plan, he promises himself.

Chapter 18: Philip Shaw junior

His buttocks are raw. Since he has arrived in Algoa Bay, after three weeks at sea, he has been in the saddle for more than twelve hours. He first thought of buying a buggy drawn by two horses but decided against it. Maybe it would take longer. He bought a big mare which looked if she could endure because he decided to ride without stopping until he reaches Colesburg. It might be that he is too late, that he never would see his dad. It was as if a fever engulfed him the moment he set foot on land. The land was the reality, the ship and sea a bad dream. He could do nothing about the speed of the ship. He simply had to let time go by. He rides the mare hard, only stopping to rest her a while, to graze and to drink water. Ahead, he knows, he will get a place where he can change the horse.

And while his behind is becoming sorer and sorer, his hatred for the three skunks is becoming bigger and bigger. He has sworn many times by himself he will let them suffer for what they did to his dad. The damn audacity of these backward Boers. What do they know of a noble character, of the gentlemanship of the English? They know nothing of fair play, of taking another being into consideration. They are people who are dependent on others for their existence; illiterate, unintelligent people! He has heard the idiom in Dutch: the tamest dog's bite is the worst. That's true: they were the nearest to him, he fed and clothed them and they bit him in the back.

He sees the farmhouse from afar just as he rides over a hillock. Suddenly his body yells out for rest, his sore buttocks for relief from torture. He looks at the sun on his track to the horizon. He dearly wants to be much further.

The farmer comes out of the house when he hears the noise of the hoofs. Maybe someone looking for overnight. Maybe another Boer on an old horse. But when he sees the horse and the rider, he realizes it is a horse of a different colour. The rider has a cap on his head and not a worn felt hat.

He waits until the young man pulls in his horse and stops in front of him. Philip dismounts.

"Rice," he introduces himself and smiles at the young man's first steps, waggling like a duck. Fresh from England or somewhere else, with soft hands and also other parts of his anatomy.

Philip takes his outstretched hand. In his best Oxford English, he greets back.

"Philip Shaw. Pleased to meet you, Sir."

A worker has already arrived to take the saddle off the sweating horse and to cool her off. Philip only pulls his saddlebags from the mare.

"You are riding her salpeter, I see," Rice starts the small talk.

"Yes, it's true. I have hoped to be much further by now."

"Let's go into the house." This is not his normal welcome to strangers. Most of the time he negotiates outside with the traveller and if one wants to sleep over, he refers him to the big barn where feed, horses, and implements are kept. This young man is different. Even the surname sounds familiar.

"Shaw, you say. Fresh from Home, not so?"

Philip looks into the friendly Scottish eyes, throws his saddlebags over his shoulders, and walks with Rice to the house.

"Yes, from England now, but I was raised here. Have been in England for four years. Studied for a lawyer."

"My world!" Rice is impressed and proud that he could judge the traveller so well.

"Very welcome here. My wife will be very pleased to hear fresh news from England. We are living a quiet, secluded life here."

"But you must get travellers often here. It's on the main road."

"It is true, but few of them are from our people." He laughs heartily and gestures that Philip must enter the house in front of him. He calls to the inside of the house and a small red-faced woman appears. They are introduced.

"He can sleep in the spare room," Rice says.

"Philip Shaw?" she asks as if she is thinking deeply. Then her face lights up. "Philip Shaw from Fort Beaufort?"

"My father came from the Eastern Cape, yes. But nowadays he farms near Philippolis," Philip answers. He looks at her in anticipation.

"Your mother passed away, let me see, eleven or twelve years back?"

"Nearer to fifteen years." Curiosity can still be read on his face.

"Do you remember, Dad?" She turns to her husband. "Philip Shaw bought some sheep from us before he went north. He said he bought a place from the Griquas round about 1862, not so?"

"Yes, I now remember. That is when the Griquas trekked to Natal. How is your father?"

"When I last heard from him he was in bad health. He had a sort of a stroke after a very bad experience with Boer children. He could maybe be at Colesburg now. That is why I race. I want to reach him as soon as possible."

"Then I suggest after supper you hit the sack. You can depart tomorrow morning at three or four. I will arrange for a good horse. You should be in Colesburg if all goes well late in the afternoon. I'm going to check if everything is okay outside. You chat with my wife in the meantime."

He grins: "And by the way, the auntie will give you some of her homemade ointment that will do some parts of your anatomy a world of good."

He finds his father in a very bad condition. Philip senior struggles to walk. His left arm hangs useless and limp at his side. The left side of his body is lame. His one eye is limp and his mouth is skew. Tears run down his cheeks unchecked when he sees his son. He can't get out a word and only hugs him with his healthy arm.

The cottage is smelling bad. Philip can see that it is not cleaned regularly or properly. His father's clothes are dirty and sloppy. He chastises the Griqua housekeeper who is supposed to care. Something is challenging in her attitude.

Who on earth gives him the right to talk to her like this. Is it not she that looks after him from the day he has become sick? She remembers well the haughty son that came home during holidays and ordered everyone around as if he was a king and she a deserting slave.

"I am working without pay," Ragie challenges him.

This takes the wind of his sails. That must be organized. His father is probably in such a state that he can't handle his monetary affairs.

"I'll pay you well," he says and takes a pound note from his pocket and hands it to her. "But get this place in order. And make sure his clothes and sheets are washed. And clean up the place."

"Who will look after him while I must go and do the washing? Here is no water."

He gets red in the face. But he also needs her help. He tries not to show it.

"You can go if you want to, then I shall get someone else to do the work and look after him." He sees his words are troubling her. He continues on a softer note.

"Please, tidy up the worst and make food for us. Then you can go. I will stay here tonight."

"Go? To where? I stay here. I sleep here." She points to her bedding and clothes lying in the corner.

This is a dilemma. He looks at his father sitting slump in a chair. He realizes his father is near his end. Maybe it is better that she looks after him and he goes to a boarding house.

He tries to talk to his father about the farm and money matters, but he only shakes his head and points with his healthy hand to a stack of papers on the corner of the table.

Philip stays until after sundown and makes sure that his father eats something. Then he takes the papers and books to a boarding house. In the light of a lantern, he studies the documents thoroughly. His father is a rich man. Apart from the farm, he has a lot of money in the bank and investments and also a formidable coin collection worth hundreds of pounds. He wonders whether the farm is well-looked after. There must still be hundreds of sheep and many cattle. Then there are the furniture, a house full of valuable antiques. And there is no debt.

There is enough money available to care for his father. There must be an old age home or a facility or maybe a private nurse that can take good care of him. He will see to it tomorrow first thing. Now he needs to rest his tired body.

The next morning very early he walks to the cottage. Ragie is sitting in front of his father's bed wailing.

Philip senior is no more.

Chapter 19: The appointment

The attorney-general of Griqualand West, Sydney Shippard, is a long man with a hooked nose, bushy eyebrows, and pale skin; also with bushy cheek beard but a smooth chin. At this moment he is leisurely sitting back in his chair in his office at Klipdrift, smoking his pipe with the long, white steel from which he now and then with timid puffs, let fly a little smoke cloud into the air.

Frequently he contemplates the future of this part of Southern Africa. The Cape's harbour is strategically important for Britain but there is no war on at this moment. To administrate this vast area under British control, now that the diamonds fields also are annexed to the Cape colony, is a mammoth undertaking. To keep it legally sound is nearly impossible.

He can understand that the Cape parliament is not keen to incorporate Griqualand West. As it is, the Cape Colony is a vast territory. Griqualand West also is huge with an enormous surface of roundabout 5 000 hectares. On the outskirts there are very little infrastructure and administration is difficult. Down south there is law and order where the people live in small areas close to one another, but as soon as you travel inland over the mountains, the country is sparsely populated and law enforcers have to travel many miles and take much time to catch only a thief who stole a single sheep. The magistrate's districts are too big. For his sense of law and order, this sort of administration is intolerable. He likes order; a society that adheres strictly to rules and laws. He likes a smart legal system that punishes those who break the law swiftly. A civilized society is one that adheres to law and order. The opposite is anarchy. He hates it.

Making it worse is the adjoining Boer republics. Rogues, so he believes, just flee over the borders and the British have at the moment no jurisdiction to follow and catch them.

He sighs, blows out the last smoke column, puts his pipe down, looks once through the window, and picks up his pen.

There is a knock on the door. The office lady enters with a fresh pot of tea. It is almost eleven-o'-clock.

"A mister Shaw is here to see you, Sir," she says when she puts down the tray on a low table in the corner and takes away the neat, white, crocheted doily from the milk jar. Shaw, he thinks, it sound s familiar. Of course!

"Please pour for us, Miss, and let Mister Shaw come in."

Moments later Philip is standing in front of him.

They greet each other. Shippard takes Philip by the arm and leads him to the table. "Let's sit down and have some tea."

Philip waits courteously until he has sat down and then sits down upright in the big chair.

"I'm so glad you are here. Your professors had high praise for you and I also received a letter from the law firm you have worked for with a good recommendation. It is a pity you have little practical experience but you will learn quickly."

"What is it that I must do for you, Sir?"

"Not only for me, young man, for the whole British empire. I want to appoint you directly as a prosecutor at New Rush. There we have so many cases of diamond theft and land claims, it seems as if we can't get our heads above the water. In New Rush, magistrate Campbell is really struggling without a good prosecutor. That means that many a rogue walks around free. Diamond theft there is the biggest problem, but also disorder, fighting especially over the borders of the claims, and serious crimes like knife stabbings, especially over weekends. Luckily you were raised here and know South Africa. You know the vastness of the magistrate districts. We are more or less able to patrol the whole area in the north, but judicial processes take too long. Criminals must sit in jail for months on our costs, and by the time the case lands in the court, the complainants have forgotten how serious the matter was, or eye-witnesses have moved away or have simply vanished. The cases are not investigated and prosecuted thoroughly, so it makes the state's case weak, and subsequently, the sentences too lean."

Philip nods. He understands this clearly. Africa is not Britain.

"The only way to curtail this illegality is firm action, thorough prosecutions, strong verdicts, and proper sentences. That would enable us to bring about a law-abiding society here in the inland, do you agree?"

Philip agrees wholeheartedly. Who is he, in any case, a rookie, to oppose the famous Shippard. Then, it is his conviction as well. After four years in Britain involved in British law, he is well-conditioned. It also satisfies his desire for revenge that he feels for the scumbags for what they did to his dad.

They chat about the problems in the area. The black workers who stream in their hundreds to the diamond fields and many who are working only to earn enough money to buy a gun and then vanish. Especially the Pedi, sent by their chief, Sekhukhuni. The problem that has emerged by allowing blacks to buy claims and also to allow them on the gravel heaps to look for diamonds. The diggers complain that this and the fact that so many blacks are smuggling with diamonds influence the prices. A further problem is the dishonest diamond buyers that are quite willing to deal on the black market and make fat profits.

"Soon, there will be trouble about these things," Shippard predicts.

An hour later, Philip leaves, heavily incited to bend the barbarism and illegality in South Africa around to slavish obedience to the civilized laws of the Crown.

Chapter 20: Emotions

Late in the afternoon, Herklaas is busy cleaning the printing machine. It is Friday and their work has been completed. Jans departed earlier the afternoon together with a group of hunters in Bloemfontein's direction. He won't be back till after the weekend.

Herklaas is happy. He knows the printer now inside out. The Dutchman is just as generous with his praise as with his criticism. His words always bring out the best in Herklaas. He works quickly, correctly, and diligently, and tries not to be a nuisance. What is more, the work and his responsibilities have given him self-esteem. He is not always afraid anymore. Also, he has turned eighteen last week and has a feeling that he is becoming a grown-up.

It is terribly hot and he has opened the door to the street in the hope of a breeze through the place. After some cleaning, he also pulls out his shirt. That's better. He reckons it would take him another half an hour to finish up. Then he would take a bucket of cold water and throw it over his body to cool off.

He is working with his back to the door and is not aware of the girl coming in behind him. He doesn't know that she is marvelled by the machinery and the racks with letters. He isn't even aware of how her eyes glide over his naked upper body, that she almost out of breath, watches how his diligent fingers relieve the metal from ink spots and fingermarks with a little cloth and some fluid. For minutes she only stands there spellbound.

Herklaas somehow becomes aware of her presence, and then he realizes that he smells something that is not the fluid he is using. It is her scent. Then he hears the rustling of her long dress in the breeze.

He turns around and wave over wave engulfs his body. First, the surprise when he recognizes her; then awkwardness about her sudden appearance; and then self-consciousness about her proximity and his bare torso.

It is Michelle!

He tries to say something but only becomes red in the face. Her hair somewhat looks a little yellow against the background of the late afternoon light. It is locks of hair bounded up by yellow ribbons. Her face is white and blushing, and beneath her eyebrows, her eyes are like small, clear, little pools of blue water.

In these eyes, suddenly jumps a sparkle of mischief. She knows very well who he is, but to intensify his nervousness, she asks: "You, Mister Wildboer?"

His tongue is like a lizard in his mouth, unwilling to co-operate as he stumbles over his feet when he turns around completely. He has lost control over his muscles. He has thought about what he should do when one of these gorgeous girls falls into his arms. He knows now! He wouldn't have done anything. His heart would simply stop pumping.

He tries to lick over his lips that have become dry like a cowhide that baked too long in the scorching sun. He grabs his shirt and plucks it onto his body.

"No, Mister Wildenboer is out." He doesn't want to talk because his voice is hoarse. She holds out a paper to him. It is Cohen's weekly advertisement that he wants early on Mondays. Usually, one of the cleaners in the hotel brings it. This afternoon it is a goddess with golden hair locks.

"Mr. Cohen …"

She hesitates. She gazes in awe. Where do you find a man who blushes so bloodred as this one? Where do you find a man that loses his senses in her presence as if she is something extraordinary? She suddenly feels infinitely flattered. She knows men. In the streets of Brussels, they picked her up as they did with hundreds of other girls, a commodity for their pleasure. No respect. It's the same as buying a piece of cake or an ice cream or a cigar to satisfy an urge immediately.

He is long and slim. He is attractive with his long, brown hair a thick bush on his head. He is enchanting with the ink stroke on his cheek. She must go, but she wants to stay with him.

He takes the paper. He wishes she would vanish to spare him further embarrassment but Michelle discovered her angel, her dearest pet, a man on which she can pour out her love unconditionally.

"Show me the machines and what you do with them, please."

Her eyes plead more than her voice. He manages to get life into his bones. Her request helps to get his mind to work and detract from his unease. He starts to talk and shows her the print table and explains how the letters must be fitted and inked to produce a printed paper. He shows her examples while he keeps on talking, and gradually he talks the lameness out of his body and the red out of his face. She pretends to be fascinated by what he says but most are lost on her, partly because she doesn't fully understand his version of Dutch, but mainly because he and his body language fascinate her to no end. His face and hands talk together with his mouth.

Eventually, he is finished. She moves closer to him, wraps her arms around his neck, and kisses him full on the mouth. Then she stands back and with a tilted head and with pouted lips she looks at him coquettishly for a moment before she turns around and with quick steps leaves the office.

Herklaas changes into a salt pillar.

Can one become so upset? This is something else than ordinary fear. It is total uncertainty. This is continually wondering. It is also a battle with his emotions. The one moment he is in heaven, the next he wants to choke in despair. Then he feels the wonderful excitement of her body, her soft lips on his mouth.

Was it an invitation or is she fooling around with him because he is so shy? Does she laugh for him behind his back?

Too afraid to come to a decision, he sits the whole Saturday morning in his room. The dancers are not doing anything this weekend, he knows. He usually prints Cohen's program for the week. They are free this weekend. It is in the middle of the month, and business is a little quieter. He has a huge urge to go to her, but the fear of probable rejection he simply can't face.

He gets goosebumps from fright when someone suddenly knocks on the printer's door. It's Chris.

"I just want to see what you are doing. Must you work?"

Herklaas doesn't answer immediately. He is in no mood for explanations.

"I was busy cleaning and tidying everything."

Chris looks around the room. Everything seems tidy and at its place. It doesn't look bad at all.

"I wondered where you are. We are all sitting in the lounge and have some drinks. This afternoon is the great wrestling match." He frowns questioningly. What's wrong with Herklaas?

Herklaas realizes he has forgotten about it. Yes, her visit this morning shifted it to the back of his mind. A wrestler from the Cape. They call him the Spinebreaker. A terrible man.

"Okay, they are all in the hotel. We are going to leave soon for the match. Have a drink, in the meantime. I'm going quickly to see Samuel. Just want to make sure."

"I'm going with you."

"No, I want him to get as much rest as possible. He is at Aletta's place and I'm going to peep in quickly. Then I will come and fetch you at the hotel. I want to see the pre-matches also."

They have already departed for the pre-matches when he enters the lounge. The place is empty except for a lonesome maiden sitting with her back to the door. She hears his footsteps on the wooden floor when he enters. She turns around in her chair. Herklaas freezes in his steps. It is Michelle. She winks at him and smiles her most beautiful smile.

"Herklaas," she says in a charming Flemish tone, " I want dearly to go to the wrestling matches. Will you chaperone me, please?"

For a moment, he considers it to turn around and run for his life but then exhilaration shoots through him. She is asking him! She could have asked so many young men. They would have been more than willing to accompany her, but she has asked him!

"You don't answer … Don't you want …"

"No, I mean, yes. I will gladly …"

"Magnifique!" she exclaims excitedly. She stands up and hooks her arm in his.

"Come, my lovely pet. Let's go?"

Chapter 21: The wrestling match

Spinebreaker, a shortish, darkish man is near as round as he is high. He has the form of a barrel with long, gorilla-like, muscled arms. His long, oily hair hangs mostly in front of his eyes. He has a flat face with bulging eyes. In his clothes, he looks like an ugly, obese man but when he takes off his shirt, you can see that he should not be misjudged. His hairy chest shows mighty chest muscles. His stomach is no fat lump but a solid mass of strong abdominal muscles.

Costa is worried. It is not going to be easy. Samuel has won the few matches from challengers way too easy because of his immense strength. Samuel has the ability to wriggle himself out of the most strenuous grips but then there must be something he can hold on to like a solid body. The Spinebreaker's body is round and slippery and Samuel will have difficulty to get his arms around him.

"Samuel, you must try to get him on his back with his legs in the air, you understand? Then lift his lower body high so that he touches the ground and press down on him. That's the only way you will get a pin, you understand?"

Samuel is quiet. Hy savours the soft hands that rub cream onto his upper body, the exhilaration thereof, and the exciting touch of the girl he loves so much. He turns his head and smiles at Aletta. Chris enters their room. He calls Costa aside.

"Have you seen the man?"

Costa nods. "I teach Samuel how to wrestle the man, but he not listen. He only has eyes and ears for that girl."

Chris smiles: "Don't worry. On the mat, it will be a different story."

Costa also hopes so. Even if he loses, it doesn't matter but he is afraid the man would hurt Samuel. Next week is this big tournament in Bloemfontein. They must take him there to make a name. If he wins there, the whole country will know of him. Then they will make big money.

"Okay, let's hope for the best. But it is nearly time to go."

Costa nods. "You go, I come."

The wrestling ring is in the big, just completed, community hall. The mat is in the middle of the floor. The spectators sit and stand around. Some brought chairs or stools. Next to the ring are a row of chairs. That is for the wrestlers and their coaches.

The unruly crowd has watched the pre-matches in anticipation of the big match. At last, the last pre-match ends.

Suddenly excitement hangs in the air like a big cloud. The Spinebreaker! Chris is convinced that most gamblers have put their money on him. There have been many discussions and arguments about the match and he could perceive their feelings. The Spinebreaker has been in town almost the whole week and in practice showed off his big bulk and mighty arms. Samuel is too inexperienced even if he is as strong as two bulls. The Spinebreaker is also an unbelievable strong man. His big reputation is that he lifts his opponent in the air, hurls him through the air, and brings him down on his back over his knee. From there his nickname. When he has executed that murderous act, he only has to fall on his opponent to get a fall. Furthermore, his long arms are strong enough to press the wind out of his opponent's lungs and so paralyzes him. It is almost impossible for his opponents to come out of his Nelson grip or head clamp.

Costa is worried because he has little knowledge of the man. How is his technical wrestling or does he rely on his strength and his difficult body. Will he try to get pins or will he try to injure Samuel so severely that he has to chuck in the towel. He looks at the man where his helper is rubbing cream on his body. To make him even more slippery thinks Costa.

The gong goes and immediately the wrestlers test each other. Each tries to get a hold on the other's arms or body but they slip out easily. The Spinebreaker has heard about this boy's enormous strength. He moves cautiously. A giant like this one can surprise him by suddenly advancing like lightning in an unsuspected move. A few times Samuel tries to get his arms around the man's body, but he slips out of the grip easily. The crowd is unruly. They want action. They want to see whether their gambles would come off.

Suddenly Samuel moves forward, grabs to the chest under the lifted arms, and tries to get his arms around his corpulence, but his grip slips and then the man gets hold of Samuel's upper arms, bends slightly, and with a mighty swing of his big body turns Samuel on his back and takes him down on the mat. With his knee on one arm and his hands on his shoulder, Samuel is totally taken by surprise.

The referee sees the shoulders on the ground and before Samuel could lift one shoulder, he taps two times on the mat. The Spinebeaker has one fall.

The Spinebreaker smiles. Even if the boy is powerful, he is too inexperienced. He will play with him until he is tired and then break his back. He savours the idea and walks to his corner with a huge smile.

Costa registers a complaint. The Spinebreaker has been smeared excessively with cream. There is no way someone can get a grip on him. The referee agrees. He orders the helpers to rub their wrestles down thoroughly. Only when he is satisfied, he walks to the centre of the mat and gestures for the gong to be hit.

Samuel is still a little unnerved by the way the fall has been won so quickly, but Costa only repeated his words in his ear: "Remember our momentum trick."

The wrestlers tackle each other. The Spinebreaker tries his trick a few times but Samuel has learned his lesson. They try with wrestling grips but have no success. The Spinebreaker now realizes how strong this young man is. Just keep on going, he thinks, somewhere he will make a wrong move, and then it is tickets with him. If he only can get his one hand between Samuel's legs to lift him for the spine break but Samuel is too elusive.

Round after round passes. They are getting tired. The Spinebreaker now realize Samuel won't tire so quickly as he anticipated. He will thus have to do his thing quickly and so win the match.

At the beginning of the next round, he moves quickly up to Samuel, clamps his one hand around his right arm, and turns Samuel's back to the referee. Like a viper's strike, his fist shoots out. On Samuel's solar plexus. He sees with satisfaction how Samuel folds double, he grips Samuel's head in a head clamp and pulls ugly faces towards the crowd who boos him.

Then he grips Samuel's upper arms, swings, and tries to throw him on the mat. Samuel feels the pain in his stomach, feels how the wind is pressed out of his lungs, feels his head clamped like in a vice, and how he is grabbed by his arms. He feels slightly dizzy but enormous anger engulfs him. He gets his left foot anchored and remember Costa's words. He feels how he is being tipped but he grabs the Spinebreaker's left arm and bends. He uses the momentum of his opponent and throws him half over his own body. He holds on tightly to the arm so that the man lands on his back on the mat with a mighty thump. He jumps on him and pins him down. Dizzy from the mighty impact of the fall the Spinebreaker remains immobile long enough for the referee to hit the mat twice.

One each. The crowd roars. It is becoming a brutal match.

In his corner, Costa sponges Samuel down. He is satisfied.

"Good. Good. Good. But now beware. He will try everything. His reputation is at stake. Watch him carefully!" He looks to the furious man on his stool. His helper is anxiously massaging him. He is hurt, Costa realizes. This is good for Samuel.

"Try the trick again. Don't engage him tightly. And mind the back break!"

The overconfidence after the last fall almost cost Samuel the match. The man is no amateur. He sails underneath Samuel clutching hands, grabs him around his head with his left arm, again turns him away from the referee and plants a might blow in his midriff. Air whistles form Samuel's mouth; without any strength, he gasps for air. Next to the ring, Costa lowers his head in his hands.

The Spinebreaker now gets Samuel's head in a vicious head clamp. For Samuel, it feels as if two rocks are pressing on either side of his head so that the little strength he had is slowly pressed out of his body. Slowly his eyes dim. He feels how this man is taking him down to the mat, feels how he is preparing to lift Samuel and break his back. Suddenly Samuel sees in front of him the most sensitive part of a man's body. If you want to play dirty …

He hits with a mighty swing of his right arm. His fist punches the target dead secure. The next moment he is free and falls on the mat, dizzy and unable to continue the fight. He only through a haze, sees Costa's face with a wide grin before he closes his eyes to prevent unconsciousness.

Only when Costa and Chris help him up, and he step by step moves to his corner, he sees how the Spinebreaker lies with his hands between his legs and how his helper throws a towel over him.

"The referee wanted to disqualify you and gives the match to him but I and others yelled at him that he hit you as well." Costa has to raise his voice to be heard.

The spectators have gone crazy. What a match! Even if there is no winner! Samuel's last fist hit was the winner! They enjoyed seeing how the Spinebreaker's eyes nearly popped out of their sockets; how his mouth opened; the pain on his big, ugly, round face; how he fell on the mat like a slain ox; and struggled to get his breath. This has been worth far more than the money they paid for entrance.

They must now frequent the hotel and the canteens. They must now relive every part of the match, every inch of it, and even put some extra flesh on the bones.

Chapter 22: Oerson

This evening Staanvas is a happy chappy. For the first time in months, he is without pain. His ribs have healed and he can move his arm freely. He feels like a new human being. The fire which around they sit has almost burnt away completely and now one bothers to toss wood on it for the fire is in them.

Cape Smoke, a cheap, devilish potent brandy is the cause of this. It runs from their intoxicated brains to their tongues which are full of wit and jokes. It is his payment for his three mates' help with the diamond smuggling. They are his confidants and tonight he treats them.

With this drinking party, he wants to tie them closer to him and the transactions they are illegibly conducting.

They hang on his lips. Stories from the Cape, of the white farmers with whom he trekked, sheep that he stole and slaughtered, girls he bedded. No one can tell stories like him, the three of them know. It is his big night tonight. When the bottle is empty, he miraculously gets another one out. They look at him with great admiration.

"The people have a big party tonight," one remarks. For a moment they are silent and listen to the mighty applause over the silent plain.

"It is Sam and the Spinebreaker," says another. He saw it on a placard and someone read the words for him.

"Let me tell you about the big fight I had with the three biggest men south of the great Gariep. Hold your cups so that I can fill up because it is a long and beautiful story." In his mind, he sees how he swings the story around so that he messes up the men instead of being messed up by them and how he set the leopard loose on them. Yes, it will be quite a story.

The men shift into easier positions. This will be the highlight of the evening.

"Well, where shall I start? With the girl with the most beautiful buttocks in the world? With the captain I fooled so easily? With the big men who chased me?"

He knows he has inflamed their curiosity heaven high. One of them waves with his hand: "Start off where you want, but come with the story."

"Now it happened like this …"

His brain warns him that he should close his mouth. He nearly wets himself and becomes sober because of fright. Silently a big man has come nearer out of the dark and joined them. Only a light flicker of a flame once lit up the man's face. It is Oerson, the biggest and eldest of the three brothers who chased him.

The men shift slightly. No one knows why he is silent all of a sudden. They move to make space for the man to sit down next to them.

"Come now! Tell us the story," one of his mates says impatiently.

"Wait a bit, guys." He tries to change his voice and moves back into the darkness. Please, let it be so that Oerson hasn't seen his face clearly, he prays. "Here is a man in our midst, a friend." He hopes his voice doesn't tremble too much. "Give him the bottle. He is way behind."

His mates laugh. They pass the bottle on until it reaches Oerson. He receives it and takes a few lusty swigs. Very nice after the hot day's walk.

"Now, the story," one insists.

Staanvas's head races. He will have to dig up another story quickly.

"Yes, tell us the one about the girl with the big buttocks."

"No man, your brains are scrambled. You have hit the bottle too hard tonight. I talked about the girl with the big tits." The other laugh exuberantly.

"Okay, it was the time when I accompanied a transport wagon to Algoa Bay. When we arrived there, I had a little money in my pocket." He hopes the distance between him and Oerson is enough for him not to become suspicious. "We would only unload the wagon the next day, so I had time for some fun. I walked down to the harbour because there, I heard, you can pick up some fun easily and cheaply for a drink or two."

He tries to get a better look at Oerson but the fire is almost down and the starlight too dim. Thank heaven it is a dark moon.

"Well, soon I saw a few sailors. Where, did I ask, are your best girls? I'm not a common guy. I'm looking for something special. Guys, I had heard that men can swear grass on fire, but what came out of their mouths was to let the sun go down. The one even reckoned that my inland balls were too small to be worth something. They were smashed, so I ignored them."

He waits and licks over his dry lips. Then he hears the blu-blup of the bottle. Oerson is helping himself. That's good! He relaxes a little.

"Very well, I was still strolling along when I see them. A very drunk sailor and the lady."

"The girl with the big tits?"

"That's right, a beautiful girl, well built and sturdy. My lust was ignited there and then. This is my girl, I thought. Then the sailor grabbed her tightly and tore away her blouse. She tried to get away from him but he had her in a tight grip. I walked up to them. He is Portuguese or something but drunk as a skunk. The girl saw me. My heart nearly stopped. Her blouse was torn wide open and guys, they sat there. I couldn't look away. I've never seen such beauties in all my life. She tried to push him away but he won't budge. Talking of pay and deliver or something like that as if he could manage anything in his state. What will I do now, I wondered."

"Give him a long blade," one of the men screams indulged in the banal story.

"No, I couldn't blade him. The police could come and take one and I had a nice work and had to look after it. I looked around. There was no one else. I saw drums where they threw in the garbage. I wanted to make sure. 'Is he bothering you?' I asked. Again she tried to push him away. 'Yes, help me, please!' she cried. Now, what could I do? I hit the sailor with the flat hand so that he flew through the air. When he stood up drunkenly, I took him by the collar and the back of his trousers and ran with him to one of the drums and threw him into the drum, head first. 'If you want to behave like a pig' I said, 'you can go and eat with the pigs.' He yelled something that sounded like Dutch Bastard."

It is time to split, Staanvas thinks.

"When I turned around, she stood there waiting for me. 'Let's go,' she said, 'I've got a room nearby.'"

For a moment the boys are silent but then they all start to talk. Staanvas is already on his feet moving backward deeper into the darkness.

"I'm going to sleep." He creeps away from the fire, away from the faint light, away from his mates, away from Oerson, a worried man.

When the first light shyly creeps over the horizon, he awakes out of restless sleep. In the dim light, he sees something and hopes it is only his imagination, or a mirage, or the aftermath of the Cape Smoke, or a bad dream. He closes his eyes. Maybe if he opens them again, the thing would have disappeared. After a while, he dares to open one eye a little. The thing is still there, sitting motionless as if it has been sitting there for ages. The thing is Oerson. Instinctively his body contracts.

"Come on. Don't pretend to be asleep. We have to talk men's talk."

Fear grips his whole body. Scarcely he is healed after they had beaten him nearly to death. Today he is going to become a corpse.

"I made sure from the men who you are."

Why not have killed me in my sleep? Why wait to torture me, he thinks desperately. His brain considers all the escape routes, but each idea hits a barrier like a tumbleweed blown against a wall.

"Oerson …"

"Shut your trap, before I hit it close for you and you spit out your teeth like mealie pips. I talk, you listen!"

Staanvas doesn't dare to say another word. Oerson sits in front of him like a granite rock against the lightening sky.

"You are going to help me. I am looking for work. Before the sun sits there …" he points with his hand to the stand of the sun at about ten-o'clock. "I want to have a job on the claims. The men told me you have excellent contacts. I'm going to lodge here and you sleep outside. And you supply me with food."

He pulls a long, thin dagger out of its sheath attached to his belt from under his shirt. With his forefinger, he strokes the sharp edge of the blade softly. Staanvas knows that knife. It is steel hard and razor-sharp. He had seen how it cut through a sheep's neck skin so that you only see blood spurts. He shivers.

"I had my say."

"I understand," Staanvas's words are nearly inaudible.

"Good. Get up so that I can lie down. That rubbish you gave me last night, gave me a headache. Awake me when you have gotten me work and made food for me. Now bugger off!"

Then I am going to stay alive, is all that fills his mind when he helter-skelter comes out of his shelter. The rest is child's play. To stay alive is the trick.

Just after ten, he awakes Oerson.

"I got work for you in baron's team."

He hands over the bottle of milk and a loaf of bread he obtained together with a few pieces of meat he paid a high price for.

"I was very difficult. They don't easily take strangers," he lies fluently. Samuel was glad to hear he's got a big, strong worker for his team. The claim is becoming deep. The hillock, Colesburg Hill, is long gone and the bigger teams now dig out their claims.

"You must start tomorrow morning."

"Why not today?" Oerson stops chewing his bread.

"They are having a meeting or something today. No one is working."

It is the day of the *tiffin* for the governor of the Cape Colony, Sir Henry Barkly. No one is at the claims today and there is a feverish commotion in the streets. Groups of diggers assemble after they have visited one of the canteens and riot and shout against the governer.

"I don't understand a thing about all this. It seems as if the English aren't in control here." Herklaas remarks.

Chris and his brothers, the baron, and the Dutchman are sitting around a table in the lounge of Cohen's hotel. At the other tables, groups of diggers are loudly discussing the situation while they wave with their arms and point with their fingers. They seem very agitated.

"Barkly is here today. All the way from the Cape. But it looks as if the boys rather want to take him by the scruff of his neck and chase him from the diggings. It's a long story." Jans puffs his pipe calmly. "You won't understand it." He points with the stem of his pipe to the three brothers. "I will fill you in …"

"Ha," the baron interrupts, "you mustn't take all day. Make it short!"

"For you, German." and he nearly pushes his long forefinger in the baron's eye, "I shall give an ass whooping you'll never forget."

"Just try it, cheese eater, I've got Samuel on my team," he jokes. "Now talk and tell them quickly."

"After diamonds were discovered here, a few groups were claiming that the diamond fields belong to them. The Free State, the South African Republic or the Zuid Afrikaansche Republiek in Dutch, or in short the ZAR on the other side of the Vaal River, and then also Waterboer the Griqua Captain, influenced by a shithole attorney, Arnot. It was a forth and back fight with words. Then the Cape Governor decided to annex the whole area, called Griqualand West, to the Cape Colony. I think it was a few days before Christmas last year. John Campbell on that day read the proclamation here and also at Dutoitspan. They appointed commissioners who replaced the old delver societies that were in charge of law and order on the diggings. With the commissioners came new rules, for example, that people of colour also have the right to buy claims, something that was prohibited altogether earlier."

"But that's not all," the baron cuts in. "I think it is mainly the illegal buying and selling of diamonds for which the coloured people are blamed, that is the cause of this unhappiness. Although the English have sent police with detectives and all, they can't catch all the thieves. The diggers reckon the old delver societies did a better job because they knew the diggers' problems and everything was more or less in order. Now it is a mess."

"And, furthermore," the Dutchman takes the floor, "here is a mix of foreigners and local people. They are not happy to be ruled by the English from the Cape. They feel England should leave the diamond fields on their own. Many feel it is just another example of English imperialism and capitalism."

The baron takes over: "In the meantime, Barkley, after opposition in the Cape Parliament, recalled the annexation. And now the commissioners are powerless and the diggers burn the tents down of the guys they suspect of doing business with the sly blacks and they hold their own courts and convictions. Do you remember the case of Charley, Jans? Right at the beginning of the year. An ugly thing."

"Oh, yes. A rich diamond dealer's worker, a white man, was accused of using Charley, a black man, for illegal diamond dealings. They wanted to burn down his place, but luckily it was stopped in time. Many others were accused of the same thing and their places were burnt down."

"Wow! But where does this tiffin now fit in?" Herklaas looks questioningly at Jans.

"Ah, the tiffin is really only an English lunch, but it is now held in the community hall and Barkly will have to explain what the government's plans are. As I understand it, it is quite a thing with a hundred and forty guests, even the ZAR's president, Thomas Burgers, is here. The mess must be resolved. I shall not be surprised if the diggers kick out the English from here completely. You can hear for yourself how unruly it is outside."

"Yes," Samuel agrees. "When I was on my way over here, I encountered a group of guys, heavily affected by Cape Smoke. They threatened to take over the police station and wanted me to help them. Luckily, I could get them back into the canteen, but it just shows you how rowdy these fellows are." He laughs. "I think by this time they won't even know which day it is."

"Yes, that cheap brandy kicks like ten horses, but ..." Jans suddenly stops talking. They hear loud cheers coming from the hall.

"Probably they have wrung Barkly's neck," the baron grins, " but don't worry. I bribed Johnson, a clerk at the bank who was invited, to come and tell us what happened."

Now the cheers have also spilled over into the streets as the news travels. A while later Johnson, a little red-haired Englishman, has to fight his way open to join them. Out of breath and red in the face.

The baron gestures to a chair and pours him a stiff whisky. "Tell!"

But Johnson doesn't seem to find words, even not after a mighty swig of his whisky. He just shakes his head and smiles. In between, he mutters words like brilliant, English superiority, clever, fantastic.

When he eventually relaxes after a second whisky, he talks so fast that they have trouble following him.

"Simply brilliant! No wonder Barkly is a sir and governor of the Cape. I've never heard such a brilliant speech in my life. He had the audience in the palm of his hand ..."

The baron becomes annoyed. "You little shit! I paid you. What did the governor say?" Johnson freeze from shock and fear: "I shall tell you. Give me another whisky."

With his fingers clutched around the glass, the story comes out. Barkly has, number 1, acknowledged that he was at fault by annexing the area. Not only are the local diggers against it, but the Cape Parliament also didn't agree with his decision. The diamond fields cannot be ruled and administered effectively from the Cape. Well, that has taken the wind out of the sails of his opponents. Number 2. The annexation thus was recalled and he will recommend to the imperial authorities to declare Griqualand West a crown colony of England. It will then be, number 3, ruled by a lieutenant-general like Natal. There will be a judicial council of diggers chosen by the diggers."

He takes another big gulp of whisky.

"Brilliant! The audience agreed and instead of jeering him, they cheered. Clever, ingenious! It saves the diamond fields for the Crown!"

Chapter 23: Caprini's plunge

Caprini is drunker than two skunks. He slumps over the counter with his head nearly on the wood in front of him. His hair that has grown long, hangs before his eyes. His hand clamps the glass as if it is a dove that threatens to fly away. It is a bad day and he is licking his wounds.

Rhodes!

He has been trying for months now to break into the circle that Cecil Rhodes and Charles Rudd built around them. At first, he thought that his approach worked for the men were not unfriendly towards him. They even showed interest in his adventures in Canada and the gold they had panned there. Rhodes even indicated that he had a vague plan to go and look for gold in the north. Caprini knew he was one of the guys on the diggings who do better than the average digger because of his eye to make a quick buck, even if all wasn't legal.

However, he is very careful. Many want to do business with him but he only does transactions with guys he trusts completely, a small group of diggers who don't transact more or less openly on the black market. These guys are also cunning enough not to sell all their diamonds in New Rush to avoid suspicion. Surrounding diggings have enough buyers, legally and illegally, who don't ask too many questions. They know that there isn't an adequate police force to curtail diamond smuggling and only a few careless guys are caught.

This morning he had a quick conversation with Rhodes when he invited him for coffee in a coffee shop. He thought he was on the brink of a breakthrough. Rhodes even remembered his name. Rudd, Rhodes' partner, later joined them. They had quite a long conversation. When Rhodes and Dunn departed, he was overjoyed. He stood up, paid for the coffee, and followed them at a short distance.

When he came around the corner of the coffee shop, he could hear Rhodes and Rudd's loud conversation about him.

"This guy, Caprini," Dunn asked. "Is it worth the while to look at him for business?"

Excitedly Caprini waited for the answer.

"I don't know. What is the talk about him?"

"He is clearly a good businessman."

Caprini heard how Rhodes made agreeing noises. His heart jumped. His ears were tuned to their finest.

Dunn continued: "Yes, clever and industrious, but I've heard he does some transactions under the table. His claim isn't that good."

"Okay then. Forget about him. Small fry," Rhodes concluded.

Caprini felt like shitting in his pants. Small fry …!

He turned around, walked to the Star of the West hotel and that is where he is still sitting this evening. Sad, humiliated, offended. That's how he feels. And that is the emotions he has tried to drown in brandy the whole day.

As if all their transactions are above board! As if they don't try to get the monopoly on New Rush! As if they are not bullying the smaller guys into selling their claims to them at scandalously low prices because they don't have the equipment to hoist gravel to the top!

It is only when the barman tells him he is closing up, that Caprini stands up and waggles to the door. Outside the cool night air hits him, not to sober him, but only to prevent that he does not in his hopeless drunkenness falls flat on his face.

He stumbles towards his room in a boarding house. He must pass Cohen's hotel. Maybe he can see her. Something tells him he is incapable to go and visit her in her room upstairs or in the hotel if she is still working. Then he sees her. She exists the hotel form the side door. She is a vague figure walking in front of him. Shivers run down his spine. This is his chance to get near her. When she reaches the foot of the stairs, he is a few yards behind her.

Chapter 24: In the court

"Your Honor, in this case, the State prosecute the accused, Samuel Strydom, of culpable homicide. Mister Strydom has on the night of 14 October 1872 caused the death of the deceased, Guiseppe Caprini, by assaulting him and throwing him down a staircase. Mister Caprini sustained a broken neck and immediate death. Witness will be led to the cause of death and an eye witness will testify."

"Thank you, Mister Prosecutor." The magistrate writes with a pen on a paper. When Philip Shaw turns around, he first looks at Samuel who sits alone at a small table with cuffed hands. Inside him bubbles a small feeling of satisfaction. This is only the beginning of his revenge, he thinks quickly. Then his eyes roam over the audience. Most of the diggers in their working clothes. What a mob! Today he will show them how British law works in a civilized society.

"I see the accused has no legal representation. I shall note that the defendant is defending himself ..."

"Your Honor, the defendant has legal representation. I am defending him." It comes over the floor.

For a moment, the magistrate is taken by surprise. He quickly looks at Philip but he also is baffled. The last he heard was that the attorney from Bloemfontein, because of heavy rains, wouldn't be in time for the case. He only pulls up his shoulders.

Somewhat irregular, but the magistrate noted the baron's details. While he is doing it, he laughs inside. Okay, Mister Baron, if you think that a pleb like you with your hereditary title can impress me and my court while making a fool of yourself, you are welcome.

"Your Honor, as the accused isn't fluent in English, I request with humility that the proceedings are conducted in Dutch or translated."

Annoyed the magistrate looks up. Is he testing my patience?

"My conviction is that the accused knows English well enough. Furthermore, as Griqualand West falls under British rule, all proceedings are held in English. Will the accused please rise!" His last words are loud to show the previous matter is concluded.

The baron smiles. He will translate himself where necessary. He gestures to Samuel to stand up. "How do you plead, Mister Strydom?"

"My client's plea is not guilty, Your Honor."

"Call your first witness, Mister State Prosecutor."

"The State calls Constable Rowan, Your Honor."

Constable Rowan is sworn in. Thereafter Philip commences with his questioning. "Constable Rowan, on the evening of 14 October you were on service at the police office. Please tell the court what happened late that evening."

"Your Honor, it was after eleven that a person came in and told me that Mister Caprini lied at the foot of the stairs on the pavement and it looked as if he was dead. I hurried to the scene. I saw him lying there. It seemed to me that his neck was broken. His head was strangely askew from the body. Luckily I remembered that Doctor Carey, the district surgeon, was in the hotel nearby. I sent someone to fetch him. I also enquired whether there were any eye-witnesses. It seemed that a Mister Bostander was the only eye-witness."

"Thank you. Your Honor, For now, it is enough. May I humbly request that if need I may recall the witness?"

"So noted. Your witness, Mister for Defense."

"Thanks, Your Honor. Constable, except that the deceased's head was askew, was there any other indication that he was pushed violently from the stairs. Did you have enough light to see clearly?"

"One question at a time, Sir!" Annoyed he looks at the baron.

"Pardon, Your Honor." The baron's face shows remorse but around the corners of his mouth flickers a cynical smile.

"I took a lantern. It is standard procedure when cases are being investigated during the night. I cannot say I saw something other than the skew neck. I didn't see anything extraordinary."

"Thank you, Your Honor. No more questions."

Philip calls his next witness. "The State calls Doctor Carey, the district surgeon."

"I was in the hotel when they called me. When I reached the place, I could see immediately that his neck was broken. On his forehead, his skin was bloody and bruised, so I deducted that the forehead hit the ground first. In any case, he was dead when I arrived."

"Would you make a judgment that he was brutally shoved from the top of the stairs.?"

"It is a possibility," the doctor answers carefully.

"Thank you, Your Honor," says Philip satisfied.

The magistrate looks at the baron and nods. With a big smile on his face, he slowly approaches the doctor.

"Doctor, can you please explain to the court in which condition Mr. Caprini's clothes was. I mean, was it torn, were buttons missing? You probably had a good look at him in the morgue, not so?"

"His clothes were dusty seeing that he lied on the ground but not notably ravaged. No buttons were missing and his clothes were not torn."

No one can make out why the baron is taking this line of questioning. Philip frowns. The magistrate looked up disturbed.

"Thank you, Your Honor. Nothing further."

The magistrate looks at his watch. It near teatime. He is thirsty and it's hot. He calls for a recess four half an hour.

Philip is glad about this. Just to make sure Oerson Bostander is ready for the interrogation that lies ahead.

When Oerson is called, he feels relaxed and assured. He knows he is a pivotal witness. Were it not for him, there would have been no court case. It is his time to get equal with Samuel. What happened that day, left a bitter taste in his mouth. It was a Monday morning. He didn't feel well at all, because on Sunday evening Staanvas arrived with a bottle of Cape Smoke at their shack. They polished the bottle. The next morning he was not able to hold a spade in his hands and the sun was too bright for his eyes. He tried to hide his incapability by pretending to work hard, but Samuel who was helping to load gravel, noticed his reluctance to work, and suddenly grabbed him by the scruff of his neck.

"You aren't working, Oerson. Are you sick?"

"Yes, Mister Samuel," he tried to hide his hangover. "My head and my stomach are not part of my body."

He tried to look up, but the sharp sunlight sent a blinding pain through his head. Samuel only had to look once. He knew what was at hand and he grabbed him before his breast.

"Monday morning hangover! You very well know what our rule is."

He knew it well. No mercy for workers who come to work on a Monday morning with a hangover for that is a major problem at the claims. There are so many workers that will be eager to take the unfit worker's place. The competition amongst the claims is intensive. The owners want to get the most out of their claims quickly. Flabby workers on a Monday morning weren't good enough.

"Get your jacket and go." Samuel was adamant. There was no choice.

Revolt pushed up in him. He, the successor of Kolbooi Visagie, the leader of the Bostander-clan. A man who is highly honoured by his people and other clans. And that when an outcast like Staanvas, a member of the insignificant southern Bastards, was more in the favour of the whites as he.

"I won't allow a henchman to push me around!"

He didn't even see the fist coming. The one moment he stood erect feeling proud and sure of his resentful stance against the white man who thinks he can control everyone and everything. The next moment a horse's kick hit the side of his face. He fell headfirst onto the gravel, felt how the blood runs over his lips. His head exploded of pain.

In the meantime, he only succeeded to pick up small jobs now and then. Now it is his chance.

That night when he loitered through the town, he saw Caprini coming out of the Star. Caprini was highly intoxicated and waggled like a goose down the street. Oerson followed about twenty yards behind him not interested in Caprini's condition.

Then, near the hotel, he saw the girl coming out of the hotel's side door. He saw how Caprini stopped abruptly. For a moment, he considered leaving and go to their shack but suddenly Caprini moved faster forward. Curiously he followed. There was a half-moon so he could follow him in the dim light.

Then it became more interesting. Caprini hastened on waggly legs. She reached the foot of the stairs unaware of the man who was following her and started up the stairs. Oerson came nearer. Then he saw Samuel coming from the opposite side out of the dark. Caprini had already reached the foot of the stairs when Aletta was halfway up. Caprini, on unfast legs, hastened after her and when she reached the top, Caprini grabbed her frock. There was an anxious yell. Within seconds Samuel with great strides hastened up the stairs. In the dim light, Oerson could only make out that Samuel slapped Caprini's hand away. The next moment he tumbled down and hit the ground with a thump. He lied still. The pair immediately vanished through the door. When he reached Caprini, he saw the man was dead. He stopped someone and send him to the police.

Only later, when there were hundreds of versions of what had happened, he decided to make up his own story. It could be worth some money.

He also remembers his conversation with Philip Shaw afterward.

"Mr. Bostander, you are a very important witness. Please tell the court what happened that night."[1]

"It was late in the evening and I couldn't sleep because of the warmth and because Staanvas snored so loudly."

The court explodes with laughter. The magistrate grins and hits with his gavel on the bench. The court settles down.

"Tell the court what happened then."

"Your Honor," he remembered Philip told him to frequently address the magistrate with these words, "I followed Mister Caprini, the girl came out of the hotel and climbed the stairs with Mister Caprini following her. I think he just wanted to talk to her. I think she was taken by surprise when she saw him because she made a little sound. Not as if she was afraid."

He looks at the intense faces of the crowd. They know his words can be the nail in the coffin for Samuel. With a feeling of importance, he continues.

"In the meantime, Samuel ..."

"Call him the accused." The magistrate interrupts sternly.

"Sorry, Your Honor, the accused came out of the dark from the opposite side. He ran up the stairs behind Caprini. They quarreled. Mister Samuel lost his temper and yelled at Mister Caprini. Then he took him around his body and brutally threw him down the stairs. He fell just in front of me like a wet bag in the dust. His neck was skew."

"Did you go closer and had a good look? Did you touch him?"

"No, Your Honor, it wasn't necessary. I could see his neck was broken and he was dead. According to me, it was from the mighty push down the stairs."

"What happened then?"

"A guy came along, maybe one of the hotel workers, and I asked him to report it at the police station."

"Thank you very much, Mister Bostander. Only a few questions more."

"Surely, Your Honor." Oerson is very confident that he did quite well. He gave the answers that Philip drilled into him quite confidently. When he reported himself as the only witness, he had one condition. Twenty English pounds. Naturally, Philip couldn't pay him in advance but promised that if he wons the case, he would not be loath to pay him.

Philip takes his time to turn the leaves of his papers to give Oerson a chance to be completely at ease.

"Mister Bostander, you have testified that you saw what happened. You have testified that the moonlight was enough for you to see exactly what transpired on the top of the stairs."

"For sure, Your Honor."

"Can you earnestly testify that there was a struggle on the top of the stairs and that Mister Strydom brutally pushed Mister Caprini down the stairs? This is crucial evidence, Mister Bostander. Would you say that Mister Strydom deliberately, in other words, without it being necessary, used violence to chuck Mister Caprini down? You understand that your answer could differentiate between an accident and manslaughter of which Mister Strydom stands accused."

"I understand completely, Your Honor. I know when there is fighting and when not. You know the accused is a big man with a wild nature. I can, in all honesty, say that what I saw was that the big man grabbed the small man and tossed him down the stairs like a doll. He landed in front of me, not like one that falls form something but one that had been violently thrown down."

"Thank you, Your Honor, no further questions."

The baron deliberates with Samuel. For a short while, they are talking intensively. The baron rises. Satisfied the magistrate nods that he can continue. Quickly he looks at Philip, satisfaction in his eyes.

The baron slowly walks up to Oerson. He bends forward. With his face close to Oerson's, he looks him straight in the eyes until Oerson looks away. The baron's voice cracks like a whip through the courtroom.

"Oerson Bostander, you are lying like a sailor!"

Philip jumps up. "Objection, …"

"Objection granted," barks the magistrate, "Sir," he can't get the baron's name in a second, "this is a court of law. Behave yourself."

"Don't worry, Your Honor. I shall now calmly question the witness."

He turns to Oerson, but maintains his threatening body language.

"Mister Bostander, on the eve of the ordeal, how much did you drink?"

The question surprises Oerson. It wasn't part of his preparation.

"I didn't drink."

"Okay, you didn't drink. You were sober completely?"

"Yes."

"And you saw Mister Caprini left the hotel?"

"Yes."

"And Mister Caprini was sober also?"

"Yes."

"You think that or know that."

"Well. If he was in the hotel, he may have had a drink or two."

"But according to you, he was sober?"

"I think so, yes."

"Mr. Bostander, if someone sits in the bar from the morning ten-o'-clock until almost the eleven the evening, do you think he was sober?"

"Objection, Your Honor. Speculation."

"Objection granted."

"Mister Bostander, if I can get at least ten witnesses that can verify that he sat in the bar the whole day and drank heavily, would you still maintain he wasn't drunk."

Oerson looks at Philip with hope in his eyes, but he looks intently at his papers. Why the questions? He can feel that the case could easily slip through his fingers.

"I will ask you this. Did he walk straight or did he waggle?"

Oerson is uneasy. What he thought would be revenge, is now becoming a nightmare. He knows he can't lie. The baron will turn it against him. He has, in any case, got a mighty fright when the baron accused him of lying.

"Maybe he waggled a bit. Remember it was dark." He looks down.

"Your Honor. I put it to the court that the deceased was horribly drunk during the ordeal. I can call many witnesses who will testify as such."

He looks at the magistrate, but he is busy with papers in front of him. He is not satisfied with the course the case is going.

"Mr. Bostander, you have testified that the moonlight was enough for you to see everything. What was the nature of the fight on the stairs."

"I couldn't see so well, but …"

"You are now lying out of two mouths. Your Honor, I am going to translate it to Dutch. The prosecutor knows enough Dutch to follow.

"Oerson Bostander, you're now lying even worse than a dentist. The one moment you say you could see everything and the next you say you couldn't."

Oerson doesn't answer. Philip Shaw stands half up to object but then sits down again.

Then the loud voice of the baron echoes through the room. "How much are you paid to lie so severely."

Oerson's eyes widen in amazement. He quickly looks at Philip, but the baron has moved in between them. Philip jumps up.

"No, I haven't been paid yet." Then he realizes what he has just said. "I mean …"

"Objection, Your Honor, …" it comes out hoarsely.

"That's okay," overrides the baron and turns to the magistrate. "Your Honor, I think we are wasting Your Honor's time and the Britsh government's money. It is clear that the witness, the only witness, is not credible. I can call witnesses who will testify to it and also there are hints of bribing. I can call the accused to testify that the heavily drunken Caprini grabbed the lady's frock and that he, to protect her, hit Caprini's arm. The deceased then lost his balance and fell down the stairs. The accused hadn't touched him except for hitting his hand away from the frock. He didn't push him or threw him. That is a lie by the witness. I request you to throw out the case."

The magistrate is red in the face. The damn German wiped the floor with them. The State's witness was pathetic. He has now one of two choices: continue with the case while the State's case crumbles or throw the case out and safe some face. Philip Shaw will have to explain! He is going to give him hell! Quickly he decides.

He hit with the gavel on the bench.

"Order in court. The case is thrown out because of an untrustworthy witness. The court is adjourned."

Everything has happened so fast there is for a few moments dead silence. Then pandemonium. The magistrate gestures to Philip that he wants to see him immediately.

Cohen rubs his hands. He can see in his mind's eye how the money rolls in. The men are going to celebrate until late this evening.

Chapter 25: Revenge

Philip Shaw is fuming. He is furious at himself. Once again, he has misjudged the damn Boers. If he could lay his hands on Oerson, he would skin him. But Oerson, according to Staanvas, is gone. He doesn't know whether it is to Bloemfontein, or over the Vaal River or back to his clan. It is no surprise because if Samuel and his brothers catch him, there will be hell to pay.

The magistrate had in his civilized, English, prim and proper way reprimanded Philip thoroughly. The court is not a place for personal revenge. It has come to his attention that Samuel is one of his step-brothers. If he had known it, he wouldn't have allowed Philip to prosecute but would have got another prosecutor. To bet all your money on one weak witness was plain stupid. He shut his ears for the bribe story for it can wreck Philip's career. Maybe it is good for an inexperienced man like him to learn a lesson from it. Pull up your socks! Case closed.

It is like gall in his mouth that the damn brothers have won again. That again they laugh at him from behind their hands. They still sway the scepter and tease him. They have muddied his prestige as one of the brilliant elects of the English in South Africa. He hated them previously, his hatred has now doubled. He must just canalize his hatred cleverly or else it is going to trounce him. He must be shrewder than they are.

Sergeant Wright. That is the solution! Wright isn't one of the young, inexperienced constables. He is over thirty and a veteran in the police service. Philip knows the diggers like Wright. Philip always thought Wright was too lenient towards the diggers. Now he is going to use him. Philip knows they smuggle diamonds. He knows that often they gamble illegally. While he is occupying himself with the prosecution of horse thieves, fighters, rioters, and such rabble, Wright will be his eyes and ears. He will gather enough information to catch them and send them to jail for a long time. And if he could get his wish, a long time in the hole in the castle in Cape Town.

A smile forms around his lips. His revenge will be sweet.

And then he hits on another plan.

Dad, I will get them!

Chapter 26: Great luck!

Imzumu is a big Zulu. He has the demeanour of an induna, a leader, proud and erect. He hates it to dig in the earth like an aardvark. To shovel gravel for a white man down under in a hole they call a claim, is disgusting. The white man has taken a gang of strong Zulus on and their claim is deeper than the surrounding ones. The gravel is loaded on wheelbarrows and pushed up the incline to the top to the sorting tables. It is washed and the diamonds are taken out. That is not part of Imzumu's work. Because he is the biggest and strongest of the gang, he must pick and spade down in the hole in the dust.

Today the devil is in him. His muscled upper body shines from sweat in the sun. His arms work mechanically. Now he hits the pick deep into the gravel, plucks it so that the loose ground hits his legs. He must work the humiliation of last night out of his system. That a small guy with a revolver in his hand and a uniform on his body could humiliate him! He, a leader amongst the Zulus, with a big kraal and many wives, only stood and shiver with inheld anger, powerless before the law.

It was Sunday evening and his men drank. They were noisy and partook in fake fights. They were unruly and executed some Zulu war dances. He sat at his fire and watched them. Sometimes he even laughed at their mischiefs. It is okay that they blow off steam, that they show their power. Then they feel they don't sell their lives to the money god. Then they don't feel like slaves. Without money, you can't live these days. You can't fight the drought and the death of your livestock. You can't buy a young, attractive, round breasted girl. You can't keep your children fat.

That is why he and his mates came.

While his men were still enjoying themselves, some of the people in the shacks nearby went to the police and laid a complaint. It is Sunday evening and they need their rest. Monday will be difficult enough on its own.

Suddenly there were three constables. Two white ones and a coloured. One of them shot into the air to bring the noise down. Then they wanted to take some of the men in custody. That's when he, Imzumu, stood up. He wasn't drunk or unruly. He wanted to talk to the police as the leader of the group. He told them he understood that they were noisy, but that is not because they are rebellious or anarchistic. This was a way in our culture to relieve tension and relax. They dance and execute fake knobkiere fights, but there is no malice in that. He wanted to prevent trouble between the police and his mates.

It was then that the policeman who has shot and still has his hand on his revolver, yelled at him and put the thing against his head, and although he is not fluent in English he could make out that he was cocky, that he rebelled against the law and that he should be thrown in jail.

His ten mates suddenly formed a line. They were a threatening barrage. If the constables would even so much as touch Imzumu, blood would flow. He was their leader, their captain, no one dare touching him.

Imzumu inhaled deeply to calm himself. His first reaction was to hit the revolver away from his head and crushed the constable with one mighty blow of his fist, but with utter control, he only lifted his hands soothingly into the air.

"My people say sorry they made noise. They didn't mean harm. I am Imzumu, I am their father. They are like naughty children, but I will tell them to be quiet. They will listen to me. No need to take anyone to jail."

"Let me tell you, you black snake. You will not prevent me from taking you in. I am tired of your barbaric riots. It is not the bush here. Here are white people also. If you once open your mouth again, I'll take you first."

Imzumu felt how gall of anger pushed up in his throat. He shivered like a reed trying to hold himself in. Never in his life, someone has humiliated him like this without his blood flowing over the ground. He quickly looked at his mates, see how their hands move to their knives. Slaughter was on its way. He had to stop it!

"Please," he tried to talk with the brown man. Maybe he understood the ways of the Zulus better than the young white constable. "Tell him we humbly apologize. I will have a hard word with my mates. They will listen. I ask humbly, please!"

The young white constable hesitates. He is afraid that the situation might develop into a crisis. He sees the fighting in their eyes. They are more than the three of them. He turns to the brown man. The brown man nods. He didn't seek his death. As deputy, he had no weapon.

"Yes, let's leave them. They won't make trouble. Let's go."

But the young constable didn't want to submit so easily. He is the law, after all.

"Tell him he shouldn't imagine he can rule like a king here. If I hear complaints again, I'll put the whole bunch in jail. Lot of barbarians!"

Out of the corner of his eye, Imzumu saw one of his men took a step forward, his hand on the handle of his knife. Like lightning, he stepped in front of the man, his hands still apologetically in front of him.

"Let's go," reiterated the brown man. He could already feel the blade of the sharp knife cutting his flesh. He shivers. Hatred! That's what he saw in their eyes. Hatred that would stop for nothing.

He took the constable by the arm.

"Come!"

Long after they were gone in the dark, Imzumu stood dead still with panting breath and clamped fists.

And now he takes out his resentment on the pick.

His mates are calling. It is lunchtime but he keeps on working. Another few strikes with the pick in the skull of the simple constable. When he looks around, he sees he is alone. He puts the pick down. He inhales deeply. He feels better. He knows he will have to leave the diamond fields soon. It is no place for a proud Zulu. He picks up the pick. One mighty blow lets the gravel spatter. He wipes the sweat from his forehead with the back of his hand and with his fingers out of his eyes.

The bright stone through which the sun shines lies perkily on the small heap of gravel. His heart misses a few beats. The size of a dove's egg, almost perfectly round. His blood suddenly rushes through his veins; his heart is a pump that wants to jump out of his chest. Initially, he wants to dive down on the diamond, but he contains himself with difficulty. He carefully looks around. No one in sight; no one is watching him. Carefully he bends, looks around again. Slowly he picks up this marvellous stone, feels how cold it lies in his palm, sees how it glitters. Then he closes his hand quickly. His mind wants to go forward, but he must relax first. Stay calm. From his trouser's pocket, he extracts a tobacco pouch. The pouch with the stone inside he puts deep in his trouser's pocket. He pulls on his shirt. Slowly he climbs the incline up to his mates. He mulls over his luck slowly and carefully.

But then his thoughts gallop to his kraal, to the open plains of Zululand, to his beautiful, fat wives and children, and slowly a wide smile forms on his face.

Maybe he should say thank you to that simple English constable.

Chapter 27: With Wright on patrol

Staanvas doesn't have any loyalty towards anyone. He doesn't like the Boers and the foreigners but he dislikes the English as well. He also doesn't like the crowds of black workers who walk half-naked through the camps. From the diggers, he steals diamonds and from the English, he steals his freedom by not getting caught. As soon as he has enough money, he will in any case get out of here. South Africa is not a place for a Baster. What future is here? No, his head tells him he should go to Angola. He has listened to may stories about that country. There are diamonds also. But there is more freedom for people of colour. The Portuguese are not as racist as the English. Over there, one might vanish amongst the thousands of foreigners and do your thing.

He also considered going north, into the ZAR, but he has a premonition that the English won't leave the Republic alone. The Republic is too weak and poor. He has listened intently when the baron and that Dutchman talked about the situation at the claims.

"The English have long arms," the baron said and spat contemptuously. "They are arch imperialists. Look what the little Arnot did with their approval! They simply took the diamond fields from the Free State Republic. The story that Waterboer was the owner of the diamond fields is simply rubbish. It is their imperialism that was behind it. And they will go north."

The Dutchman agreed with every word.

"Yes, and look at what is going on in the rest of the world! There is no country that has a piece of richness that they don't take over."

"And no one can stop the red pigs. The German Kaizer is a clown. The French's legs became thin and weak. Who else can stop them?"

"Yes, you are correct," the Dutchman continued. "Russia has internal problems and has no interest in Africa. On how long the Germans will hold out in East Africa, is an open question."

No, Staanvas thinks, not where the English have their tentacles. Then better the Portuguese. He will have to make sure he has enough money. It is going well with his business. Just a pity about Caprini. Caprini and he had many profitable transactions. Staanvas himself often went to the surrounding diggings to sell diamonds. Mostly small ones but once or twice some big ones too. The black market network is well established and reasonably safe. All of his contacts are very careful not to land in jail.

That is why Staanvas got a fright when sergeant Wright, just after his supper, suddenly appeared at his shelter. Even with a small bottle of quality brandy in his hand. Wright doesn't look like someone who is on the point of taking someone into custody.

"Staanvas," he says while he hands over the bottle, "I don't take any liquor but this one someone gave to me. You may have it."

Suspicious and reluctant he takes the bottle. Then he pulls a drum nearer for the policeman to sit on. But the sergeant holds up his hand.

"No, I don't want to sit. I'm here to commandeer you."

"To what?"

Wright bursts out laughing.

"You are not in trouble. You must go with me down the river. Trouble between Bushmen and a group of Kora has been reported. The Bushmen brought a complaint. The prosecutor promised he would send someone. So, I must go but I don't know their languages. The magistrate suggests I must take someone along to help me communicate with them when or if I encounter them. I must commandeer him and he will be sworn in as temporary deputy constable. You will even get paid for it."

Staanvas's mouth is dry. His brain cannot comprehend this sudden thing. It must be a trick to catch him. He will carefully decline.

"I don't know …"

"It's no trick, Staanvas. I know you don't have a permanent job. I know you are familiar with the Kora and can understand the Bushmen. That's why I've chosen you to go with me and translate for me if necessary. And frankly, I would very much like it if you accompany me. We are short of hands to investigate all the cases. So, what do you say?"

What can he say. Wright has thought about everything.

"And if I don't want to?"

The sergeant laughs. "Rest assure. The magistrate can order you as Colony citizen, but I don't want you to join me by force. You are a civilian, so I ask you as a volunteer to go with me. I need you, please."

Staanvas can only nod meekly.

"Be at the office of the magistrate tomorrow at eight. You will be sworn in. Man, think about it, from tomorrow you are under the protection of the State. You naturally will get one of the fat police horses to ride on."

He greets and turns around and walks away with long strides. He smiles. It is going to be sports. Otherwise, it is very monotonous in this dry world. The diggings with its thousand of men have its own problems. It is not a normal society. There are no real families, maybe here and there under the rich. But mainly it is loners, fortune hunters, adventurers. And thieves, crooks, and scallywags. These people mostly believe in their own laws. The law of survival. The law of an eye for an eye and when they are drunk, an extra eye and some teeth with it. The jail always is overfilled. Mondays after the fines for drunkenness and fighting, the jail is emptied. Only the most serious offenders remain behind bars.

And sometimes on a Monday, they find a corpse or two. Most of the time killed and cut up with a knife. The offender is dead, no one knows about it and you get no witnesses willing to testify. It is the law of nature. The strongest, the fastest with a knife, the most agile and cunning survive.

And many Monday mornings up to half of the workers are absent from work. Stomach ache, headache, dizzy in the head, maybe wounded in fights, cut by knives and they stay in their shelters or shacks or tents, not only the blacks and the coloureds, but also the white rabble. The diggings throw together quite a mixture of people.

Wright is still smiling. He doesn't like Philip Shaw much. The man is haughty and thinks he is important because of his studies in England. He is thankful for the recess from the diggings and rubbish of the diggers. He is looking forward to his trip. He is already planning to take longer than necessary. Will see how it goes down.

Chapter 28: The Pofadders

Staanvas is delighted with the Wright's slow pace. He has ridden years ago and he knows your behind can get quite sore. They only travel on a light gallop and he must say the saddle under him is an excellent, English saddle. Maybe his buttocks would hold.

They are going in a south-westerly direction. Somehow they will come across the Riet River. Somewhere along the Riet, he thinks, they should find the group of Kora if you can believe the Bushman's story.

About ten Wright rides in under a batch of camel thorn trees. The crowns of the trees join and make a nice shade. He climbs down and takes his helmet off. Sweat drops forms where his helmet rested on his head. His hair is short, reddish and white head skin shows here and there on his scalp.

He gestures to Staanvas to dismount, then he takes from his saddlebag a flask of tea, biltong, and biscuits. They take the bits out of the horses' mouths for them to graze. They sit down, Wright with his back against the trunk of a tree pouring tea into two cups.

"Well," he laughs, "in Engeland eleven-o'-clock is teatime, but we take ours a bit early. To ride through the open plains in this heat is hard work.

He hands over the cup and biscuits to Staanvas.

"Nice, these farm biscuits," he says as he dips one into his tea. "You know, I like South Africa. I don't think I want to go away from here back to England."

Staanvas is silent. He is still in the dark about this whole outing.

Wright shifts his helmet rearward and with his eyes on the horizon, he continues leisurely.

"The only thing I really hate is this damn helmet. It makes my head sweat profusely. And it is hot here in the north. The Cape is better. But I don't complain too much"

Staanvas, suddenly interested, wants to know about England and Europe. He is sitting on his haunches his hands folded around the tin cup. The biscuits he dropped in his pocket.

"Surely quite different here than in England."

"Oh yes, vastly different. But I can't think I will easily adapt to the cold and the little sunshine again. You know, before I came to South Africa, I had to patrol London's streets. *Bobby on the beat*, they call it. Day or night you must patrol your sector, past stinking rubbish and monotonous, brown double-storey dwellings that all look the same. In wet weather, in snow, or in the narrow streets that threaten to smother you, the heat brewing entrapped in between the buildings, the damp of the streets they sprayed in your nostrils. Now look, how nice it is here."

He stares over the veld. Blond grass plains as far as your eyes can see.

"But how about Europe. How does it look there?"

Wright frowns. He doesn't know really. People of his social standing don't travel. He hasn't even seen much of England. Many people don't even leave their cities or towns in their lifetime. He only knows there are big and smokey cities. He also knows that vast areas of the countryside are owned by the rich. They only use hired employees to work the farms for them. Some of them even are now on the diggings. He has no intention to talk about this.

"Here are a lot of Europeans on the diggings. Talk to them. They wouldn't be here if it were so wonderful in Europe."

Staanvas is not satisfied with his answer. He is looking for gum to stick his new dream together. The talk about England has opened new horizons. Why not go back to his roots? Why not go to France?

"But over there there aren't whites and browns and blacks? Not slaves and servants."

Wright grins. "You are looking for Utopia. But you are right. There are not many people of colour. Slavery have been abolished years ago. But there is another system that keeps some on top and others down. Social discrimination. Upper, middle, and lower class. And this is a system that keeps you in your place, maybe even more so than this racial discrimination. Look at me who comes from the lower class. I shall not advance to a senior position in the police. Earlier, I don't know if it is still happening, rich fathers bought ranks for their sons in the police and the army, even if they were not the right material. But I'm satisfied. I'm still young. Maybe I will advance to major. I think I can forget to become a captain one day."

He scratches his head. "But tell me about yourself. I can see you are not from this area."

Staanvas doesn't show his surprise. During the years he has learned to experience emotions without showing it. Wright gestures for him to hand over his cup. He fills it.

"I'm really glad to be away from New Rush. I'm quite fed-up with the snooty Shaw and the magistrate Campbell who thinks this is small England. This is altogether another country. They will not last long. But tell me!"

Staanvas don't really want to talk, but the atmosphere is so convivial and when he starts, the words bubbles over his lips. He must say, he rather likes Wright. Sometimes it is good to open up and it really can't hurt anybody. His real name is Stavast Senaymont. Stavast soon became Staanvas. He tells Wright about his youth, his grandfather who was French, how his father kicked them out, his transporting days and how he eventually ended up in New Rush, but nothing of his big love for the girl with the fantastic buttocks.

"Yes," the sergeant reacts after he has listened intently, "I could see you are not the average digger. I feel you have seen and experienced more than the workers on the diggings. I am not surprised that you can read, write, and do arithmetic."

Staanvas wants to reply to that, but the sergeant stands up and quickly walks to his horse.

"We must get going."

Two days later they reach a bend in the river. A few branch shelters and a few sheep and cattle indicate a sort of settlement. Barking dogs greet them. It is in the middle of a scorching day and the inhabitants all are in the shade of their shelters. Staanvas knows they will only come out very late this afternoon. It is not a good time to bother the people, he thinks, but whether the sergeant has something in his mind about it, he doesn't know for he is silent.

"Good afternoon, people," Staanvas calls, unsure about which shelter harbours the leader.

The sergeant wants to dismount, but Staanvas gestures with his hand to stay put. There suddenly is a feeling of danger in the air. Even the dogs have stopped barking.

He is quiet for a long time watching each shelter for the faintest movement.

"What are you looking for!" the voice cracks behind them.

Staanvas plucks his horse around. First, he sees the gun that is aimed directly at his chest. Then he sees the cruel face with raised knife cuts behind the gun. And next to him he sees a very long man with a gun trained at the sergeant. Wright has also turned around, his hand on the way to his revolver holster, but instinctively he knows pulling his gun would be futile.

Staanvas has been frightened to such an extent that he can't get a word out.

"Tell him," the sergeant's voice is hoarse. "Tell him not to shoot."

Staanvas gets his voice back. "Good day, my brother. Don't shoot. The sergeant and I are on patrol."

"What are you looking for? Where are you from?" The voice is harsh and unfriendly.

Staanvas's legs shake. He's been told of these individual Kora gangs. They first shoot and talk afterward. They don't acknowledge the English administration and also no other authority in the north-west. It is also not easy to catch them when they were unlawful for they are constantly moving. He must say he has not expected to come across one of these groups. It is clear that the man with the injured face won't wink an eye to kill them.

"We are coming from New Rush. We got a complaint from a Bushman, but I see here are no Bushmen around."

The last part he added quickly in the hope that it will cool down the crisis. He sees a little tolerance in the eyes of the man and he relaxes a bit.

The sergeant also sees it. It is as if the gun that was so precisely pointed at his breast, is moving a little lower. "Tell him if there are no Bushmen nearby, we have got no trouble. Tell him I've got a bottle of brandy in my saddlebag and we would like to share a drink with them to show our friendship. Tell him we have travelled a long distance and would like to rest for a while until it is a bit cooler."

Staanvas translates. For a moment they don't react.

Then the leader starts a long conversation in the Nama language with the long man. Staanvas doesn't understand a word. He only sees how the long man fervently turns his head to the leader and make incomprehensible noises. At one stage the leader points with his forefinger to the long man. Then he gestures to Staanvas and the sergeant to dismount and follow him to a big camel thorn tree. He gets down on his haunches with the long man next to him and gestures to Staanvas and the sergeant to come and sit next to them. Staanvas goes down on his haunches but the sergeant sits down on his buttocks after he has fetched the bottle from his saddlebag.

He unscrews the bottle and hands it over to the leader. The leader takes two swigs that bring tears to his eyes and hands over the bottle to the long man.

"I am Anneries Pofadder. This is Tiny Jakop." Jakop nods and gulps a hefty mouthful and hands the bottle to Staanvas. Staanvas only takes a small sip. It is wise to be very careful.

Staanvas repeats the names for the sergeant.

"Pofadder? Never heard such a surname. Does it mean anything?"

"Pofadder, in English puff adder. Very important clan along the river."

"I am Staanvas. I'm also from this area in the south." He waves with his arm. "And this is sergeant Wright from the police at New Rush." He passes the bottle to the sergeant who also takes a small swig.

"Ask him, before we go any further, whether they have seen any Bushmen lately." The sergeant again passes the bottle to Anneries. Staanvas translates.

Anneries takes the bottle, lifts it until it is in front of his right eye, stares with one eye as if he can see through the brandy to the sergeant. Staanvas's heart wants to stop. He knows this is make or break time.

Then Anneries slowly shakes his head from side to side. "Way back there were a few that try to steal our sheep, but we chased them off."

Satisfied the sergeant nods. He knows the story. The instigator frequently brings the complaint. He also knows what chase away means. Probably they have hit and tortured the Bushmen.

"Tell him, I understand. No problem. How many are here." He points to the group standing in front of the shelters with mouths that yearn for a swig of brandy.

"Not many," Anneries answers quickly. Staanvas knows that many of the men, women, and children hide behind bushes or rocks. Luckily the sergeant knows when to stop prying. He only smiles and hands over the bottle, now in his hands, to Anneries. Something is wrong! He has experienced this feeling many times in his years of policing. He sees it in Anneries and Little Jakop's eyes. He reads it in the threatening composure of the people in front of the shelters standing in a half-circle.

He rises very slowly and smiles his friendliest smile to Anneries. "Tell them we are quite happy that they did nothing wrong. We are going now. They must enjoy the rest of the bottle."

Staanvas is still slowly coming upright when suddenly a hellish cabal breaks loose in the shelter the furthest from them. Many things start to happen simultaneously. The group rushes to the shelter but through the line slips a bushman, nimble as a rat. He runs to Staanvas's horse. Sergeant Wright immediately understands what is happening and pulls his revolver from the holster.

"The horses, Staanvas!" he screams. Then he jumps two yards to the right and aims his revolver at Anneries. Anneries and Little Jakop have either from the brandy or the surprise, not moved and their guns lie harmless next tho them. Wright whistles for his horse who comes running up to him and in one movement he jumps in the saddle while still covering Anneries with his revolver.

Staanvas's horse neighs and anxiously steps around while the Bushman runs to him. Staanvas and the Bushman reach the horse simultaneously and Staanvas grips the horse's reins but he is on the wrong side of the horse. The Bushman has already jumped and got hold on the saddle. Startled the horse starts to run away past the group that now dazed stands in front of the shelters. With all his might, Staanvas clings to the reins and tries to run alongside the horse but he stumbles over a stone, the reins slip out of his hand, and he falls down.

Immediately one of the young men from the shelter draws his knife, a long, sharp dagger, and runs to Staanvas. The sergeant realizes that the horse with the Bushman hanging from it is lost to Staanvas. Luckily Anneries and his mate haven't moved yet. They know if they move, they will be shot.

"Here, Staanvas, come jump on my horse!" he yells while he slowly turning his horse around so that Staanvas can jump onto its backside. Staanvas has difficulty standing up. He had a mighty fall and is dazed. Then he comes to his feet and tries to get away from his pursuer as quickly as possible. There is little chance that he can reach the horse before his pursuer is on him. The man is nimble and quick. He is upon Staanvas with a few strides. The blade flashes in the sunlight almost against his back. Then the young man lifts his arm. The hand of the pursuer remains for a second at the highest point.

The shot rings out. The young fellow follows Staanvas for a yard or two then he falls in the dust, a lead pill in his upper leg.

"Come!" Wright yells again and lets his horse move forward. He feels how Staanvas bangs against him on the horse. Then he kicks the horse in his flies. If they can just get away far enough before Anneries and Jakop shoot at them with the guns. Luckily there is a bunch of sweet thorns and they go through the trees. Shots are fired but it is too hasty and wild. The bullets whistle through the top of the trees. Then they are through the bunch of trees. Only a lucky shot can hit them now. In front of them, now on a jog, they see Staanvas's horse with the Bushman still clinging to it.

Wright bursts out laughing. The tension of the arduous ordeal is gone. The danger is past and the whole thing is funny for him. They ride up to the Bushman and get the horse to a standstill.

Staanvas mounts his horse and lets the Bushman sit behind him. Then they ride with a strong gallop for about half an hour.

"Wasted a whole bottle of brandy," the sergeant laughs when they stop next to the river to let the horses drink and make something to eat and drink for themselves.

"Can you speak to him?"

The Bushmen understand the language of the area. He tells his story.

They ambushed him. He was on his way back from New Rush to his own little group when they caught him and bound him up. They tortured him even more than the first time. He doesn't know where he was hit but his whole body is sore. When he heard the voices outside, he wriggled with inhuman effort out of the rawhide thongs they had tied him up with. And what previously had happened was that they came and chased the Bushmen out of their shelters. When he, who is the leader of the Busnmen clan, tried to oppose them, they first bound him up, tortured him, and then chased him away. He has heard that the English are now occupying the territory that's why he went to New Rush. Where is his group now? He doesn't know exactly but he will find them because when they ran away, he screamed after them to go to the place where they camped last year in the winter. It is in the Karoo. He'll get them there.

"What now?" Staanvas is flabbergasted. Police work is difficult. What will the sergeant do now?

"Nothing doing. Here is no case. Ask him whether he wants to lay a new complaint."

"He says he would rather like to go to his people. If we have some food for him, he will hasten to his group. He wants to get away as far as possible from the Pofadders."

"But now the Pofadders?" Staanvas asks.

"We won't see them again. I suppose it was not the main group. They are as far as I know, lower down the river. This was only a splinter gang. They are going to hide in this outstretched land. It will take years to catch them. And the police are short of men. No, no case. I shall report as such."

Two days later they see New Rush at a distance. It is late in the afternoon, but the heat still lies like a blanket over the bare, rocky plains. The sergeant stops under a big, lone pepper tree.

When they sit relaxed with cups of coffee, Staanvas says: "I have to thank you for saving my life. That guy nearly put his blade in my neck. I already felt it all along my spine."

Wright holds up his hand. "It is what a guy must do. If I didn't like you so much, I would have let him cut off a biltong." He laughs heartily at his simple joke.

"But seriously now. How do you like police work?"

Staanvas smiles by himself. Eventually. The whole trip was a foofie.

"It's okay," he answers while turning the cup around, "especially when you get paid for it."

"Hmm," the sergeant reacts. "Say you can make a lot of money for a deputy constable. As you have told me you want to get away. Say you can get a lucky break!"

"I don't know," Staanvas answers carefully. Where is this leading?

"Let me be honest with you. You are a clever man. You buy and sell diamonds illegally. It can cost you dearly. We know most of the handlers. The problem is you must catch a smuggler redhanded when they are doing a transaction and to catch one doing business without a diamond license."

Staanvas knows exactly what he is talking about. The smugglers are shrewd and have many foxy plans. There are smugglers with diamond licenses like Caprini had been. Who can guarantee that the diamonds didn't come out of his claim? Diamonds aren't marked. The smugglers hide it in the most unbelievable places. Swallow it, stick it in the anus, in their hair, and where else.

"And the punishment is harsh. Easily eight to ten years hard labour depending on the magistrate. And soon, I have heard, there will be a proclamation to regulate the whole police force of Griqualand West. Even the detectives also. I hear guys from the Frontier Police of Kenhardt will be stationed here. They want a proper police office and force to keep law and order and to curtail illegal diamond dealings."

Staanvas is silent. He supposes the sergeant will now come to the end of the story. "And," Wright continues, "I hear Inspectors McLean, McKenna and O'Connor are coming to New Rush. They are hardy policemen."

"I don't understand …"

"Listen, you stay on as deputy. No one has to know. You help us capture a smuggler. We trap him redhanded. The prosecutor wants to make an example of him. You vanish. To Cape Town, Durban, Algoa Bay, overseas, wherever."

"Who?"

"Can only tell you when you agree. Or else you might tell him."

"I understand."

"Think about it. In the meantime, you remain a deputy. You don't have to do anything. Only be our eyes and ears. Spy a little but don't touch anything illegal." He laughs loudly with a wide-open mouth. "Just remember. As soon as we have more police the smuggling will stop and the jails will be full of them."

He takes out his pipe.

"Let's have a smoke to round off our trip." He takes out his tobacco pouch, fills his pipe, and hands it over to Staanvas. Staanvas shakes his head. His mind is trying to get around the sergeant's words and warning. He must contemplate whether it will be good or bad for him.

"You know," the sergeant says while he blows out smoke like a steam engine, "I think I know you better than you know yourself. Me and you, we are so …" He points his bare forefinger up in the air. "Loners. Lone wolfs."

Staanvas's thoughts become even more entangled. Maybe he didn't realize it so sharply in the past, but it becomes clear now. Even if Wright may deny it, he has just given away that he is as lonely as Staanvas is. Yes, they are loners. Islands in a sea of people. The sergeant needs a friend, a partner, even if it is temporary.

Staanvas is still sitting and gazing over the blond plains when the sergeant stands up.

"Let's go. The trip is finished. Before evening I want to have my report ready." Staanvas smiles. He knows it will only be a few lines.

It is the other thing that bowls his existence over. France. He has seen many Frenchmen at the Cape. Even darker than he is. His granddad was French. His colour won't be a doom over there. In this country, his own country, he is degraded to a second class citizen. He doesn't fit in somewhere. He is not a Griqua. They have now their own land. One group in Griqualansd West an another in Natal, under the leadership of Adam Kok. They also have their own land, Griqualand East. He could maybe fit in with the Basters. He has heard of a group in Rehoboth in the German-occupied country, South West Africa, but for even a drier land than this, he has no appetite. No, on a ship to Europe! To France! To his roots! Senaymont. Senaymont.

For this, he will have to pay a heavy price because he already knows who the target is. He can't get his head clear. His mind stands still like the wheels of a wagon which break blocks have been fastened too tightly.

Chapter 29: The brother's fight

Herklaas is furious. He has been arguing with Chris for more than an hour.

"Listen, Chris," he tries once again, "it seems to me you don't want to understand!"

"You are wasting your breath. I know what I do."

"You can't know, because Philip sits behind this thing."

"Now tell me if you know more than I do."

"But you must listen and listen carefully."

Chris shrugs his shoulders.

"This is not only about you. Get the bigger picture in your mind. Samuel and I are also part of this thing. Samuel has already been in court although he did nothing wrong."

"And I ..." Chris wants to make a snotty remark but holds himself in.

"Listen, let me tell you straightforward. I despise the underground activities that you are involved in. They all know you are rogue."

Chris stands up. Who the devil do Herklaas thinks he is. Where does his bravado come from? Not even Samuel dares talking to him like this. What happened to the little boy who always wanted to wet his pants?

"Are you finished? I am going now."

Herklaas has also stood up and is now standing in front of Chris threatening him.

"Sit! You and I are going to talk things through!" Chris is stunned. It looks as if Herklaas is ready to attack him. Slowly he sits down.

"Listen, again what you don't want to understand is that what you do throws a reflection on me and Samuel. We are your brothers. Behind your back, bad things are told about you. Do you think it is nice for us to hear that? And further ..."

"Are you not finished yet!"

"No!" Herklaas exclaims. "I have always listened to you. Today you are going to listen to me."

"And further. Anita clandestinely overheard a conversation between Philip and sergeant Wright. They were having lunch at a table near the stage. She was behind the curtains and they didn't see her and she couldn't hear everything clearly. But one thing she was sure of was that your name was mentioned frequently."

"Those two are pumpkins."

"Don't be so sure. If they catch you, you are going to jail. Is that what you want? There is another thing. You know Philip wants our blood. Do you want him to win? Hasn't the thing will Samuel taught you anything? He is not going to rest before he gets one of us, or even all three of us, in one or other predicament. And you want to give him the opportunity. I'm asking you with tears in my eyes …"

Herklaas doesn't know how right he is, Chris thinks. He knows he is being watched. He knows his days at the diggings are becoming short. And Herklaas is correct: Philip won't be satisfied before he has avenged his father's death. And yes, he knows he embarrasses his brothers but he has his plans worked out. Only one big transaction and then he's gone overnight. This rock that he bought from the Zulu, gives him the final opportunity. And then north to the Zuid-Afrikaansche Republiek. Gold! For the last time, he plans to score big.

"Okay, Herklaas. I hear what you say. Only once more. I'm going to make a big hit. Then I'm on my horse and gone. Don't worry. They must try to catch if they can."

"You are too self-assured. Maybe too careless. The last time could be the very last time," Herklaas answers pessimistically. Only the fact that it was the last act of smuggling, helps to soothe his mind a little.

Chris has by now counted every stone in the wall of his cell. He knows exactly how many yards its breadth and width are and it is not many. Entrapped like an animal as they say. And this by his stupidity. He should have listened to Herklaas. He should never have trusted Staanvas. With Caprini long forgotten, he had to look for a trustworthy contact.

He smiles bitterly. He decided on Staanvas. And all went well. Many smaller diamonds and much cash have changed hands between them in the last few months.

Then came the Zulu. They were all standing and looking at the baron's last sieve's washing. He felt a light pluck on his arm. Next to him, the big Zulu moved in. Just for a moment, he opened the palm of his hand. By the bound up pouch, he could see it was some stone. He nods slowly and around the mouth of the Zulu a smile flickered.

"Horses," he said nearly inaudible. The Zulu nodded. The appointment was made.

How the man hit upon him, he would never know. How the man knew about the swap place, is beyond him. It is at the stables of the post coach. The two Griquas that are the stable masters always, for some money of course, hid the smugglers behind the horses, saddles, bridles, and feed at the back of the stables. They also functioned as sentries while the deals were done.

Just before sundown when there is much movement around, when many workers walk to their homes and the horses are brought to the stables, the smugglers slip in. Within minutes diamonds and hundreds of pounds change hands. Unobtrusively, secretly.

The Zulu was there. I the dim light of the space at the back he took out the diamond. Chris couldn't believe his eyes. Thousand pounds he immediately reckoned. It was huge and as far as he could see, pure.

"Two hundred." He took out the notes and started counting. Usually, this trick worked with inexperienced smugglers. They only see the money.

"Aikôna. No."

Chris holds three fingers in the air. The Zulu smiled. Zululand calls.

Klipdrift, he thought immediately. He will have to get someone to sell it for him there. Seven hundred and fifty pounds they must get. Six for him and one and a half for the seller. Not a penny less. A fat amount for both.

The rock burnt in his pocket. It was big money and your sentence will be lengthy if you are caught. He should only use someone he can trust completely.

A few days later, he saw Staanvas in front of a shop.

"I'm going to Klipdrift soon if you have something," Staanvas said when they pass each other without looking at Chris.

Chris then knew. Staanvas was his man. He trusted him. Quite a few men are trading on the black market, but they play with small change. This one is another gem. The carrier can just as well sell the diamond and vanish with the money. Therefore, security must be built into the transaction.

A few days later they passed each other near the claims.

"Tonight eight-o'-clock behind the Star." Chris made an appointment.

He had to wait more than half an hour before slowly out of the dark Staanvas moved towards him.

"Feel him. He is pure."

Staanvas felt. It was big.

"How much?"

"Seven fifty, not a penny less."

"Okay, I'll take him."

"No, no cheating. What do you have?"

"A few smaller ones and two big yellow stones."

"I'll keep it until you return with our money, okay?"

"You don't trust me?"

"Just as little as you trust me. We help each other."

"Will let you know where and when we exchange."

The dark swallowed Staanvas. He was satisfied. It would be a good transaction. Since Philip has arrived on the scene, he knew he and his brothers will have to move eventually. This is going to be his last transaction.

Ride with your horse before sunrise with the road to the west. I shall get you about two miles out of town, Staanvas let him know with a courier a few days later.

Five-o'-clock he was in the saddle with a hired horse. Slowly it was becoming lighter in the east and he could identify the veld and the trees around him. A clear, cloudless day. A good day for business.

Suddenly Staanvas was in front of him. Left of them were a few flat thorn trees and next to the road was a dense cluster of buffalo thorn trees. He dismounted and they greeted. Staanvas had a broad smile on his face.

"Let's turn to the east for more light so that I can have a good look."

"No. Show me yours first."

Staanvas laughed heartily. "I won't cheat you."

He got his pouch out and shakes his stones onto the palm of his hand. Chris could see it was not bad stones at all. He was satisfied. Staanvas rolled his stones back into the pouch and held it in his hand. He gestured.

"Good," Chris said and took out his pouch, took the diamond out, and held it between his thumb and forefinger against the morning light. Staanvas whistled.

"Wow! What a beauty!

"I'll take that!" Wright's voice came from right behind them. A constable came from behind the bush aiming his revolver at them. Chris felt how nasty shivers ran down his spine. That was his first sensation before the reality of what just had happened hit him in the gut.

"And put your hands behind your backs. And no jokes. Resistance against the law may be very dangerous." Wright took both pouches from them.

As easy as that!

Now he is sitting here. What happened to Staanvas? That he was outwitted so easily, gives him a very bad taste in his mouth. Even worse is the thought that Philip Shaw now has the upper hand. He also struggles with other questions. How did Wright know? Staanvas had been there already. Did Wright apprehend Staanvas first and then waited for him? Could Staanvas be part of the ambush? He looked so at ease, not if a barrel of a revolver was aiming at him.

Thoughts are swirling through his mind. He is in custody until his case comes before the court. No visitors. No bail. The magistrate reckons it is a serious offence.

Chapter 30: Betrayal

The night breeze is cool on his hands and face. He holds the reins lightly in his hands. The moonlight and the well-used wagon spoor ensures that the horse calmly and sure of his steps gallops lightly.

What has passed is in the past, he thinks again. He seeks in his heart for remorse of what he had done. Turn the thing on its head, he argues with himself. Chris transgressed the law. I was the law. I was a deputy constable in the English police force. It was my duty to deliver him, to let them catch him. Would he have felt anything for me if the shoe was on the other foot?

In fact, Wright had me nicely in a corner. If I hadn't worked with them, he would have apprehended me. I had too little chances in my life to be locked away in jail for many years.

Now get this out of your head, Stavast! You are not part of this land. Your history lies in France. Over the sea in Europe. The rest was in the East. Only a small piece sits in this damn land. His mother had been so proud to be connected to the French. And your name from now on is Stavast. A good French name. Get the notion that you are a baster out of your head and heart. His heart becomes lighter and he sighs the tension out of his body. The exhilaration of a new life, a new beginning, starts to bubble like a small fountain inside him.

An hour later the horse gets a fright from a little antelope running across the path. He whinnies and jumps wildly. Stavast who is half lulled to sleep by the even gallop of the horse, gets a fright and he has to grab the saddle not to fall off.

He suddenly pulls in the rein. The longer he thinks about it, the more unsure are his plans. East to Bloemfontein? Then to the north around the land of the Basuthus? Then to Natal to Durban and aboard a ship? They told him they were always short of skilled hands. But Natal is English and the English may perhaps wait for him. They have a very good postal service and mounted postmen where the coaches don't travel. The Cape is English, Algoa Bay is English, Durban is English. Long before he can get to any harbour, news about him could have reached there and when he wants to board a ship, they might apprehend him.

And that telegraph! That thing sends messages all over the country very quickly. Before he reaches Durban, he could have been declared a fugitive. Why would he trust Shaw and Wright? They themselves are rogue.

Maybe it was not such a good idea to take the diamond.

After they were apprehended, Wright and Chris departed.

"Constable," he ordered," bring the other captive." He laughed. "Please make sure he doesn't escape."

The constable waited until Wright and his captive vanished over the nearest hillock and then unlocked Staanvas' cuffs.

"You were brilliant!" the young constable said admiringly. "How you could remain so cool-headed ..." He shook his head.

Staanvas remained silent. The case of the reward lied ahead. He didn't trust Shaw in any case. He could change his mind as easily as a jackal can jump around.

Shaw and Wright were in the police office. They shook Staanvas's hand. They were delighted. It was going to work like this, they explained. They have already bought a horse and a nice saddle and provisions for his journey. Did he want to go to his shelter? No, he has already sold it to another man and took the money he had hidden there. Now they want an affidavit from him about what transpired. Wright and the constable will testify in the case. His absence when Chris is in court is called witness protection. Therefore, the affidavit. Shaw handed him a handwritten document which he signed.

He had to stay in the charge office until five when Shaw would bring his money and then he can go. By that time the streets would be busy and he could easily depart unnoticed.

It was a long day. He settled down on a hard, wooden bench in the small office and tried to get some sleep before his long nightly ride. He was almost asleep when a tiny fellow came into the office and walked to a funny gadget in the corner with a paper in his hand. Seconds later the thing clap-clapped like a small hammer on an anvil and he jumped up. Carefully he walked closer to see what the hell the man was doing. When he was finished the little guy explained to Staanvas how the thing works. Of Morse code he understood nothing, but what stuck in his head was that what the man tapped in on the gadget are carried by wire and can be picked up by another machine on the other side and deciphered. Much better than the postal service, the man joked. The signals are transferred by wire and arrive at their destination almost immediately.

At five they were there. They were alone as Wright had despatched all the constables to patrol. Wright and Shaw with a bulging purse of three hundred pounds of English notes. His horse was saddled and ready outside. They thanked him again. Wright unlocked a drawer of a cabinet and took out both pouches. Then he opened the one with the big stone and took it out. Staanvas was already moving in the direction of the door but he stopped. He saw how Shaw took the stone from Wright, held it up, and admired it while smiling broadly. It hit Staanvas like a rockfall. With him out of the way, no one can testify which diamonds were smuggled. They still have the other pouch. Clever rascals. They were surely planning on keeping the big diamond for themselves! He even had a liking for Wright!

Suddenly there was a hellish commotion outside. Five diggers were pushing another in front of them yelling at him.

"I shall kill the swine!" one of them thundered in a loud voice. Wright and Shaw quickly went to the door, but only after Wright returned the pouches to the drawer that he locked and hung the key on a peg against the wall.

The office was empty. Staanvas hesitated just for a moment. Then he rushed to the wall, got hold of the key, and hurried to the cabinet. He unlocked the drawer and quickly got hold of the big diamond. He locked the drawer and returned the key.

He could hear the digger shouting when he slipped out at the backdoor. "The shit has dug under our claim and it is a mess and all the gravel is down under in his claim." It will take quite a while to sort this one out, he knew.

He got onto his horse and rode away. When he came across a long a string of workers coming from the claims, he saw Samuel. He nearly ran him over with the horse.

"Samuel," he could get out hoarsely, "take this. It belongs to Chris."

Then he turned his horse and kicked it into a wild gallop and fled east.

Now his nerves are shattered. Unsurity clamps his soul. What if they catch up to him? How long will it take before Wright realizes that Staanvas bedeviled him? The night that at first was his friend has now become a scary enemy. It feels as if his thoughts bounce back from the dark. It is as if the horse can feel his tension through the reins and it becomes jittery. Soon it gets startled by a rabbit. It swerves and again nearly throws Staanvas out of the saddle. He pulls up the horse and stops. His heart bounces in his chest.

He gets a terrible fright when he hears a horse's hoofs. From New Rush, someone is coming on a hasty gallop and he doesn't spare his horse. Can it be Wright or a constable hot on his heels? Or a post rider? Can they still catch him or has he passed the border into the Orange Free State where they can't apprehend him?

He dismounts and pulls his horse into the bushes alongside the wagon spoor. He waits with inheld breath. The sound of the hoofs is ear-deafening. Scarcely five yards in front of him the horse and rider race passes him. He cannot make out who the rider is. It could well be a constable.

His nerves are shot. The strain of the day, from this morning, up to now is simply too much. Suddenly he knows what to do. Get away from the English! He climbs on his horse, turns in a north-easterly direction, and on a very slow trot, he rides through the veld.

Chapter 31: What now?

The four of them are sitting in the lounge of the hotel at a table.

"What is going to happen now.?"

Aletta is terribly upset. For a long time, everything has gone well. She has her work as a dancer at the hotel. Samuel is the boss of the baron's claims and then he takes part in wrestling matches. He is now the country's champion. On the diamond fields, in Bloemfontein, and Pretoria, there is no match for him. Even in Port Elizabeth, the old Algoa Bay, there is no one. Once they went to the Cape and he had a few matches and won every one of them. They don't stay in the attic anymore, Samuel bought a brick house from an Englishman who quitted and Chris is staying with them. Herklaas is still working for the Dutchman and they have extended both the lodgings and the office. Herklaas now stays in a comfortable dwelling.

It seems to her that everything is now turned upside down. She looks at Herklaas.

"I don't know what now."

The old fear and insecurity that he has left behind a long time ago seem to rush up and overwhelm him. He shakes his head.

"When is he going to court?" Michelle sits on the edge of her chair. She is dismayed to see Samuel and Herklaas so worried and in a bad mood. She can understand it. Chris has been their leader and planner for many years. He was the one that paved their paths. He took care that no one bothers with his brothers because he had money and he had friends. His network in the smuggling den has always been secure and safe.

"The date isn't set yet. I don't even know if magistrate Campbell will preside. Maybe he waits for another magistrate. Or maybe the snake of a Philip Shaw has yet another trick in his arsenal."

"I heard they want to catch a few smugglers more before they set a date." Michelle hears many stories because during the day they help as waitresses when the lounge becomes busy. The men drink and talk and she listens.

"Are they also talking about the jail? In other words, where will he be jailed when he is found guilty?" Samuel takes a big swig from his ice-cold beer. Herklaas shivers at the thought of jail for Chris.

"There is another possibility," Aletta says, "I hear talk of taking him to Cape Town to be prosecuted there. In any case, I think he will be moved to one of the big towns or cities. The jail here is too small."

Herklaas whims. "It mustn't happen!" he called out dismayed. "It will be the end of him!"

"That he let him caught like this!" Samuel looks over their heads with a frown between his eyes. "It's Philip Shaw's work. But what must I do with the diamond?"

Herklaas frightens. His stomach turns.

A long and heavy silence hangs over them.

"What did Staanvas tell you, Samuel?"

"We must use the money to get him released."

"Then the diamond must be sold," wheezes Michelle. For her, this is a new world opening up. It is dangerous. She gets goosebumps all over her body. It's exhilarating!

"Let me think about this," Herklaas takes the lead. "You two must please hold open your eyes and ears and look for a safe contact."

"Oh, that's not difficult," Aletta jokes, "you just must not become too jealous."

"And if he is a Casanova, it will make the transaction so much nicer," Michelle jokes with and hooks her arm around Herklaas's neck.

Herklaas don't even try to react to their teasing. He stands up. "We'll have to make a plan pretty soon. We don't know when he will be in court."

"And what then?" Samuel looks carefully around as if he expects someone to eavesdrop on them.

"I don't know. I must still think about a plan." He hits his fist against his forehead. "Let's go."

Potchefstroom.

There is a commotion in front of the office of the South African Police Service. Many young men, some still in their saddles and others next to their horses, are noisily chatting. Some sway their guns through the air and shoot imaginary shots.

War! The Pedi! Exhilaration floods through their veins. They are coming from different commandos and are here to report for enlisting in the army. On one side there is also a group of coloured men. They also want to be part of the oncoming war. Only a few of them have horses and of course, they have no weapons. They are no less excited than the group of white men and they are as noisy.

Stavast can see the crowding from afar as he rides down the street and he is baffled by it. Are they getting a commando together to catch rogues? Or do they want to go and attack the Free State like last time with the Winburg affair?

He nears them slowly on a light trot. With his new clothes, saddle and bridle and his new gun slung over his shoulder, he looks like an important man. If someone did not pay too much attention to his skin colour, he could easily be taken for a young white farmer or Boer. At Hoopstad the Jew made sure he bought nice new clothes and the barber next door took great care of his hair and the little stumps of beard he has. He looks quite distinguished.

A Field Cornet comes through the door of the office and standing on the veranda, holds his hands up in the air. With difficulty, he succeeds in getting some silence.

"Men," his voice sounds sharp over the commotion still going on, "I know you are here to enlist as soldiers, but everything is not arranged. I have orders to take the names of volunteers. This is not a general call on the commandos to enlist."

"That is why we are here," a big, sturdy boer yells from the crowd, "we want to enlist!"

The morning air thunders from screams and the Boers wildly sway their guns in the air. The Field Cornet gets a smile around his mouth hooks.

"I'm very proud of you," he screams, "but be quiet now so that we can do this thing orderly. Once again, you must understand clearly. This is not a general call-up to go and fight the Pedi. There will be no war. Not against the Pedi, the Zulus, the Swazis, or any other group. The case is this: every sector must organize its commandos. I am going to write your names down. Each one will then get a slip to get some ammunition from the magazine. But, and this is the important thing. The government wants to establish a force that they call the Border Police. Its task will be to patrol the borders of Swaziland and Zululand and prevent all undermining activities. Their biggest task will be to establish order in the north where the Pedi raids have become a nightmare. When we are through here, those who want to join the Border Police must get a form from me and fill it out to be selected. Do you understand?"

"Oh, no!" the big guy screams. "Is that all? I have thought …"

"Yes," the Field Cornet tries to explain, "I know stories were taking the round of a war against the Pedi. It was obviously wrong …"

"Then I have wasted my time. I do not incline to ride patrol for nothing." His voice thunders over the crowd. He walks to his horse and he takes the reins. "Another wind egg from the government, ba! I am going."

He mounts his horse and plucks him around. He gallops away. About half of the crowd follows him. A dust cloud follows them.

"Please men, make a queue here," the Field Cornet continues unfazed. "We are going to use the office inside to write down your names and also a slip. Without that proof, you will not be able to get ammunition. It must be picked up at the magazine down the street."

It takes a while for all the men to tie up their horses and form a queue.

"What about us?" calls a long, slender brown man from his group.

"Yes, you must also form a row. We can use you as after riders, chefs, or whatever. Let us take your names also." He indicates with his hand where they should form a queue.

His eyes roam over the groups. He is looking for someone to help him write down the names. He sees Stavast still sitting on his horse. Very neat, this man. Surely he can read and write.

"Sir, what is your name?"

Stavast first looks around to make sure the man talks to him.

"Stavast Simond."

"Aha, a beautiful French name. I commandeer you to come and help me write down the names. Fasten your horse over there and come into the office!"

Stavast at first wants to get annoyed. It was not a request but an order. Who the devil does this man think he is to commandeer him? However, he must acknowledge that the man doesn't know he is not a citizen of the Republic, but a Cape subject. And if he now refuses or seems unwilling, the Boers won't tolerate it.

In the roomy office, there are two tables with utensils and paper.

"Stavast, please write down the names of the brown men. I should have had an assistant here but there is trouble on one of the farms nearby and the police are out. Thanks, in the meantime."

"They don't get slips because they don't have weapons."

"Correct." He is impressed by the insight of his helper.

"Okay, let's start."

The first men come in from a row like a snake from the table going out the double doors down into the street.

They start.

"Hendrik Lodewyk van Staden, Mooiwater, Kommando Voorslag." The Field Cornet writes down his name and then the printed slip. The farmer holds it high like a flag of victory.

"Witbooi Klaas, from the shacks just outside Potchefstroom." Stavast writes.

About halfway through the queue, they suddenly hear the hoofs of a galloping horse. Moments later a young man, red in the face, rushes into the office. He is panting.

"Field Cornet," he shouts distressed. "You must come and help! Some guys are instigating chaos at the magazine. They want ammunition! They don't want to hear that they must first register. They don't want to listen. They want to break the place down. I locked up, but please, you must come and help to prevent big trouble!"

"Stavast," the Field Cornet immediately decides. "Take over form me. You can later finish your row." Then he calls out loudly. "I want a few volunteers to come and help us!"

Soon he has a group of ten men. Stavast shifts to his table.

"Alewyn Burgers, Zoetevlei, Kommando Voorspoed."

He writes it down and also writes out the slip.

It is going well. He has about twenty names on the list.

"Etienne le Cordeur, Vlakplaas, Kommando Vlakplaas."

Stavast writes.

"Are you really a descendent of the old French reverend Simond that they got for the French Huguenots?" the young farmer wants to know. He is very proud of his French surname.

Stavast's heart suddenly gallops like a young horse. He has a vague plan but if this inquiry wrecks it, what then? He will have to take a chance.

"Yes, as far as I know, but I've never had such an interest in my forefathers, but earlier I was in the Cape. Le Cordeur, in any case, is a beautiful French surname."

The young man wants to ask further questions, but he is pushed away by a sturdy man. "You can unravel your families later on. I want to finish up here. My farm is waiting." Stavast has difficulty to get his breathing under control.

Eventually, only a few men remain. He leaves a line open before he writes down the next name. He prays the Field Cornet stays away long enough.

Eventually, the last man. Then he acts hastily. In the line he left open, he writes Stavast Simond, Schoongesicht, Kommando Fleur." He hopes his premonition is correct that the list is only for control of the ammunition being dealt out.

It can change his whole life. He also writes a slip for himself.

Then he shifts to the other table and calls the next brown man.

Chapter 32: Constable Wilson

"There is not much we can do about it." The baron shakes his massive head before he takes a massive gulp of his beer. "He brought it over himself. He must take what comes to him."

The baron and Jans Wldeboer sit at a table in the hotel's lounge. Jans drinks gin and beer.

"Yes," he laughs, "we all know who are rogues here on the diggings, even the big guys that press the smaller ones into the corner to sell cheaply, are robbers. The secret is not to be caught."

"That's true," agrees the baron, "now that the claims are becoming deep, it is only the big guys with machinery who will survive. Last month William Hall even got the first steam engine on the go to drag the gravel from the deep claims. I have bought some claims from poor strugglers who have no money for equipment. But I paid them reasonably well."

"I know your 'reasonably'," Jans jests. "You have probably sold those claims for a 'reasonable' price and put plenty *rijksdaalders* in your pocket."

"Cheesehead. These days we are talking in pounds, shillings, and pennies. The English have taken over long ago. Poor old President Brand's complaints were fruitless. He had to take the few pounds the Lord gave him. They are not going to leave the ZAR alone. Gold in the north, I hear. Near Pietersburg. Just you watch!"

The Dutchman shakes his head.

"But what does the English want to do there?"

"Listen, the Republic's money matters are dire and the government unstable. This is a good time for the English to take over. Remember, they still have this confederation plan in their heads to get the two Boer republics, Natal and the Cape under one administration. Great imperialists they are."

"But the Free State Republic won't play along."

"I'm not so sure. If you can get three parts into one confederation, the Free State might be forced to play along."

"Well, maybe. Before they became independent they were a British sovereignty."

"Just wait and see. You and I are already under a British administration. We are now a Crown Colony."

"Yes, it will come sooner or later. You know that old Queen Victoria has been named the 'Empress of India.' What does this tell you?"

"As I've said, imperialism runs deep in the English."

"Wait, I see Chris's brothers and their girls are coming. Let's go. I don't want anything to do with it."

"Well, Herklaas works for me. In a way, I am involved."

"But keep your nose out of their plans. They will have to look for an excellent advocate."

Constable Wilson is disgusted. What should have been leave, is now work. What pleasure and joking should have been with his friends and his colleagues, is now standing guard. He himself has overseen the erecting of the big tent because of the expensive equipment and the probable looting of temporary workers the company had to employ. Wright was in charge and he wanted nothing wrong. Everything had to be executed orderly and precisely.

Naturally, it is the consequence of his success in capturing that Strydom guy and a few smugglers more, that he now thinks he can throw his weight around.

Wilson spits on the ground. He knows exactly why Wright has chosen him to guard the prisoner tonight. Not because he is inefficient in his job; he is a good policeman. Not because it was his turn, he should have been on leave and free. It is because of Anita. It is about that lovely, dark-haired dancer. For months he has tried to carefully seek rapprochement. He knows in his neat police uniform, he is an attractive young man. He ascertained when she was on service in the lounge and then had lunch and made sure she was serving him. At first, she had difficulty with English, but he considerately offered to teach her for free. During his free afternoons, he taught her in the hotel.

When they were sitting intimately at a table and she was learning words he had written on a piece of paper and he shyly held her hand, and she promised to call him Basil, Wright with his big ass and big voice entered. He stopped, watched then intently, a deep frown between his eyes, walked to a table, and ordered a beer. Wilson was surprised but also anxious because he was familiar with that look and frown. And when Anita talked about the friendly sergeant who also frequently talked to her he knew, it was plain green-eyed jealousy. He never thought Wright would change the service schedule and take him on his free evening out of circulation with the order to go and guard the very important prisoner at the newly built jail cell. Because the building is not completed, adequate security wasn't yet in place and this gave Wright the excuse to change the schedule for this circus evening and place him as a guard in front of the cell away from everything.

And now he is standing here. More than an hour already, while he can hear the music coming from the tent and can see in his mind's eye how the people are streaming to the tent. There is a stool on which he can sit but he is now too resentful to do that. He rather walks to and fro while he tries to calm down his turbulent mood. At half-past seven someone brings food for the accused. He lifts the lids and stirs the soup to make sure there are no weapons in it. For him, there is a very nice cooked meal. One thing about the Boer women; they can cook. Just look at all the corpulent men over fifty.

Too soon the supper is finished. Their tin plates and cups are taken away. He makes sure that the cell door is firmly locked. He puts the key into his trouser's pocket.

It is dark. The night has thrown his black blanket over the place. No moon. Only the stars that try to sparkle bravely in a cloudy sky. He tries to see through the dark but eventually, he can't even make out the bushes in front and not far from the cell. They haven't yet cleaned the area form bushes, shrubs, and trees.

He sits down on the stool. The loud music from the circus tent comes in waves through the quiet air. A trumpet sounds from afar. Basil hears the screams of applause from the spectators. He knows the first clown has appeared. He tries to imagine he sits on the stand with his arm around Anita's waist; she cuddly close to him. And they laugh. But somehow he can't get the reality of a bitter taste in his mouth and the hatred like a wall around his heart, out of his mind

"Anita," he whispers. He forces the picture of her lovely body and sparkling smile out of his mind. He turns the lantern down. No sense in lighting up the vicinity. The dark is now his friend. It helps him to keep his thoughts in check. He sighs. Then over to mental gymnastics.

His father taught him that. To concentrate deeply and relax. To avoid thinking of bad things when you have to do bad things. His father learned it in India. He starts to concentrate. The music fades. The picture of Anita subsides. The hated smile of Wright is gone. He is on the Scotch highlands.

He runs through a patch of flowers. He plays in a shallow stream. He tries to catch small fish with his bare hands. He smiles. He lets the images roll by slowly to pass the time. He lets his head rest against the wall behind him. The images fade. He is half asleep. The minutes pass.

The voice floats softly through his haziness.

"Basil. Help me."

He smiles. It is Anita's voice. The voice seems far and unreal.

Then it comes again. This time a little louder.

"Basil, help me, they are hurting me!"

Maybe it is his imagination. The haziness subsides. He stares into the dark in front of him.

Then he hears it clearly. A shuffle like someone who is struggling to get away from someone. The groan of the girl wrestling someone.

"Basil, help!" This time it is clear and loud.

He grabs the lantern and turns it higher, lifts it high to see in the dark. Vague figures dance just out of the light's circle so that he cannot make it out clearly. Then again a hard groan: "Basil!"

"Anita!"

He rushes forward but the sounds have moved deeper into the darkness. Quickly he darts forward with huge strides. Strong hands grab him from behind. The lantern plunges to the ground. A pillow is pulled over his head. He wants to scream but the breath is being pressed out of his body. His arms are caught in the grip around him. He wants to kick but his feet are lifted from the ground and then he feels how his feet are bound up. He feels the black darkness in his head and then nothing more.

When he regains consciousness, he discovers that he is bound up tightly. His hands are bound behind his back, the pillow fastened tightly around his neck, his feet pulled up behind his back and tied to his hands. Then he hears it. The sound of horse's hoofs galloping away. His stomach turns. Although everything is black before his eyes, he sees it clearly. The captive has fled. He only will be relieved in the early morning hours. By that time Chris will be gone for hours, even over the nearest border. It is less than an hour's hard ride from here with a good horse. Then he could be in the Orange Free State. There he can vanish or go to the north.

The terrifying consequences agonize him the most. Dishonorable dismissal? Jail time? And the humiliation! His clean record muddied.

Whatever the consequences, he will look for him. He will get him! There will be hell to pay! He will take revenge!

Two dark figures slip into the hotel through the side door.

In their room, they start to giggle heartily.

"I like Africa," whispers the girl with the long, black hair.

Chapter 33: North?

Before six Wright stands in the office of the Dutchman.

Herklaas emerges from his room, only half-clothed with sleep heavy in his eyes.

"Where are your brothers!" It is not a question.

Herklaas wipes the sleep out of his eyes and yawns.

"As far as I know, Sergeant, Chris is behind bars. Of the whereabouts of Samuel, I can give you zero information. Saw him only yesterday early afternoon. Maybe at his home. Why do you ask, Sergeant?"

"Where were you last night?" The voice is harsh and the words abrupt.

Herklaas plays ignorant: "Why, Sergeant?"

The sergeant has no desire to play games. He tries the bullying technique. He is sure it will work with this guy.

"Come, my man. Let's not play games. Where were you?" His voice is loud.

"Since yesterday evening I have only been here, Sergeant. I worked. Do you see that pack …"

"You lie, man! I know you were not here the whole night."

"Then, Sergeant, you know more than I do. Ask my boss. I was here when he came back from the circus."

"Why didn't you go to the circus?" Maybe he can trap him with this question.

"That is a personal matter, Sir, but if you must know, my girlfriend had a nasty headache, she gets migraine, you know? So we stayed at home. As far as I know, her roommate volunteered to stay with her in the hotel the whole night."

This is exactly what Michelle and Anita have told him. But it comes too easy. It is too concocted. But how to prove it. Chris is gone. Samuel is gone and his girl also. All that Wilson can recall is that he heard something in the dark like groaning and wrestling, that he went to inspect and was grabbed and bound up. Wright knows that Anita wasn't out. She refused to accompany him to the circus.

He is upset with Wilson. He is upset with himself. He should have deployed two guards. He is going to be castigated. The hell will be loose. Shaw and the magistrate won't spare him.

"If you are finished, Sergeant, I would like to get dressed."

Wright is flabbergasted by the bravado of the young man. The boy who has always scuttled about like a shy mouse suddenly changed into a cheeky cock. There is nothing he can do about it. He will say in his report that he suspects Samuel for Wilson's apprehension and that he freed Chris. What else? He has no other suspects. Maybe as little information as possible in his report. And no wild speculation. It can only make their humiliation greater. In any case, the smuggler that he so cleverly caught is gone due to his and Wilson's ineptness. If there were any collaborators, they have vanished as Samuel did.

He sighs, turns around, and leaves the office with hanging shoulders. An ugly day lies ahead.

It is at beginning of December 1872.

The bar on the square in Pretoria is a rather small room. Not that it really matters. Even if they are sitting shoulder to shoulder after a long workday, they are drinking and socializing with fervour. Their conversations cover only one topic. The escalating problems between the ZAR and the Pedi. Sekhukhuni, the Pedi chief, now has a formidable army with guns which were mainly bought by workers on the diamond fields and brought back. They debate the question of whether the so-called border police force would be a deterrent big enough to quell the unrest on the ZAR's borders. Further, they quibble over who is going to enlist and who not.

"But their order will be to patrol and further do nothing! It is useless and a waste of time! We must take them on in their nests before they get more weapons." The young man takes a healthy swig of beer. His mate must dug away from his swaying arms.

"I've heard they have a plan to smuggle canons in. And President Burgers wants only patrollers." He sniffs noisily. Others agree dismayed and noisily.

"They won't get away with that. Only now Burgers has no spine. If a man like Kruger were the president. It would have been a different story. Wait and see ..."

Stavast is sitting at the counter with a beer and is amazed. It is not only what the men say, it is how they say it. They only temporarily accept the state of affairs. There is a mood in the air, there is an expectation, there is a will, a determination to turn the situation around, even with force. These are men that have something to fight for and they are more than willing to do so. He experienced the same attitude in Potchefstroom.

He doesn't want to be a part of it. He hasn't yet figured out what he is going to do, but to be caught up in a war is not part of it. He sits and drinks his beer and listens to the arguments, jokes, and squabbles. That is enough, for now.

Suddenly a heavy hand rests on his shoulder. He looks around. Chris's brown eyes look straight into his.

He wants to say something, but his vocal cords aren't playing along. His speech organs are out of order. Then he forces himself to get control.

"Chris," he tries to talk over the noise of the bar, "we must talk." Chris gestures with his hand to the outside. He nods. What must happen, must happen.

The air is cool after the stuffiness of the bar. Chris points to the square. They start to walk.

"Chris …"

"Thanks for the diamond," Chris cuts in.

"The diamond?" he asks flabbergasted.

"Yes, the one you gave to Samuel."

"Oh, that?" Suddenly the picture changes. He is still feeling like a traitor, but to think of it, yes, he has paid for his betrayal of Chris.

"Yes that, Staanvas …"

"May I interrupt you for a moment, Sir." He stops and turns to Chris. "You are now talking to a certain Mister Stavast Simond. I have French heritage, but since a few days ago I am also a burgher of the ZAR." He takes out two papers. One is the proof to get ammunition with which he walked to the landdrost's office and told the clerk he wanted to join the police force but he wasn't officially a burgher. He showed him his proof to get ammunition and a few minutes later he was registered as a citizen of the ZAR. "And I don't know a person named Staanvas. Maybe he is dead."

Chris has an imbecilic expression on his face. He looks at the broad smile on Stavast's face. Eventually, it dawns on him.

"You devil!" he starts while the words and their implications are sinking in. Then he bursts out laughing. "Goodness! You did it!"

Stavast also laughs. Chris put out his hand. "Pleased to meet you, Mister Stavast Simond. If you ever come across a guy named Staanvas, please tell him the diamond was sold for a stack of money. And tell him, because you wouldn't know my brothers, that my one brother, the wrestler and his wife, are also in Pretoria where they plan to open a hotel. My other brother remains on New Rush. Maybe he can start his own newspaper or magazine there."

Stavast still holds Chris's hand in his. He presses it softly and lets go.

"And you are now a proud citizen here," Chris smiles again. "Your plans?"

"To the east. I aim at the Portuguese if I don't settle here somewhere. I actually want to go to Europe, to France, back to my roots. But I have to make more money."

"My idea precisely. Make more money. I've got a little. And we must make money. Much money and then come what may."

Stavast frowns. He doesn't understand why Chris refers to 'we'."

"What do you know about Eersteling?" Cris looks at Stavast questioningly.

"Eersteling? Never heard of it. Mind you, a farmer on trek had an old cow that calved. He called the calf Eersteling."

"No man, we are not discussing cattle. Eersteling is a place near Pietersburg where an Englishman, Dutton is his name, found gold. That is the first discovery of gold in the north."

"Thank you, but no thank you. I'm not a man who likes digging in the earth after diamonds, gold, or whatever. My plan is …

"Listen, Stavast. We are not going to tunnel like moles in the ground. We are businessmen. Look, you and I have money, not much, but enough. What do the diggers want? Think about New Rush."

"The first is a canteen and then a place to stay …"

"You are not so dumb as you look," Chris jests. "Precisely, we are going to open a tavern. Drinks, food, and lodging. We will make a fortune. Think about Cohen in New Rush."

Deep in thought, Stavast stands motionless without any emotion on his face. Chris waits patiently. Eventually, Stavast smiles.

"North!"

"So, it's north," agrees Stavast. "The idea is growing on me."

"Now then. What are we waiting for? Where is your horse?"

They walk over the square in the rays of the sun low on the horizon.

ABOUT THE AUTHOR

Gert van Jaarsveld is a retired professor in Linguistics after a successful academic career of 25 years. He also has years of experience in translation, editing, proofreading in English and Afrikaans. Since 2018 he is the editor and translator of the serials and other content in The Free Story Magazine. He also is a published author of short stories, novels and articles. His eBooks features in the Story Magazine's Bookshop.